MURDER

ON THE

SAN GABRIEL

A Fen Maguire Mystery

MURDER ON THE SAN GABRIEL

A Fen Maguire Mystery

BRUCE HAMMACK

Chapter One

F en sat at the kitchen table, wishing he'd gone to the cafe in town. Mornings like this made him consider wearing noise-canceling ear buds from the moment he pushed back the covers until he climbed back in bed at night.

He shot a quick glance to Thelma, his cook and house-keeper. His reward for looking at her was a broadside of accusing words. "What are you looking at? Your bacon and eggs will be ready when they're ready and not a second before. I swear, between you and Sam, I might as well tell the funeral home to come get me."

He made the mistake of allowing a low moan to slip out and instantly regretted it.

"What was that?" She wagged a bread knife at him. "If you don't like the service, speak up."

He raised his hands as a signal of surrender, attempting to blunt her words. "No complaints."

She chuffed something unintelligible.

Fen placed his hands on each side of his coffee cup and

kept silent. His mind, however, wondered if something was wrong between Thelma and Sam, his ranch and farm manager. How could he broach the subject without her coming at him with either the knife or a pan of hot grease? He took the coward's way out and let her rant until the storm passed.

The gale of complaints shifted direction but seemed to grow in intensity. "Where's Bailey? I can't stay chained to this stove all day. If that gal sleeps any longer, she'll get cold eggs and biscuits that won't melt butter."

Fen ventured into the fray. "She stayed up late working on a sketch of an owl."

"Why is she ruining her health by not getting enough sleep? Who in their right mind wants a picture of a stupid bird?"

"Lots of people. Wildlife sketches sell very well."

"I don't know why anyone would waste good money on such a thing." Thelma tore a paper towel from a roll and wiped sweat from her face. Her next question had an accusation built into it. "Who was that interrupting your time with Sally this morning?"

The mention of his late wife's name caused Fen's heart to clench. Every morning, no matter where he was, he talked to his wife's photo. He swallowed and answered in a low voice. "It was Chuck. He wants me to come to his office this morning."

"Don't go," said Thelma with ire in her command. "That lawyer is nothing but trouble. You know what's gonna' happen, don't you?" She answered the self-posed question. "He's going to tell you someone got murdered and you'll travel to some town halfway across the state to help the police find the killer."

Thelma waved the tongs she was turning bacon with at him. "Let the police do their job and you stay where you belong."

"I'd like to, but I can't, and you know why." He didn't elaborate, nor did he need to.

Thelma turned back to the stove and mollified her tone but not without a complaint. "Ten years as a highway patrolman and another ten as sheriff should have been enough."

"I made a promise," said Fen.

A sleepy voice sounded from the doorway leading into the combination kitchen and breakfast nook. "What promise?" The question came from Bailey, the nineteen-year-old budding artist who lived in an apartment over the garage.

Fen answered the young woman's question. "I made a promise to Sally before she died that I'd not become a recluse artist. She knew I'd want to stand in front of a canvas all day and she was right. If I don't break up my routine, the world becomes small and meaningless."

Bailey tilted her head as she settled into a chair at the table. "Now I understand why you're still solving crimes. It also explains why we travel to sell our paintings and caricatures. You need to get out."

Thelma let out a huff. "I hope you two realize I don't sleep worth a flip when you go chasing after cold-blooded killers. I'm praying lawyer Chuck and his wife Candy have something else in mind."

Bailey's eyes opened wide. "There's a case for us? Super! Where are we going, and when?"

"You ain't going anywhere," snapped Thelma. "Fen made the promise, not you."

Bailey eased out of her chair and moved toward Thelma. "What's wrong? Your face is red and you're sweating."

"That's because it's hotter than the hinges on the gates of Hades in here."

Bailey looked at Fen, who returned her gaze with a confused look. He countered Thelma's claim of the room's temperature. "Thelma, it's February and there's a heavy frost this morning. You're standing over the stove, but look at what Bailey and I are wearing. A Carhart coat for me, and Bailey has a full-length robe over her pajamas. She's even wearing a wool cap."

"Don't forget the alpaca socks and new house shoes I got for Christmas."

Fen acknowledged the addition to the list. He tried to see the thermometer in the backyard, but frost on the windows obscured details. He took a different tack. "I passed the thermostat on my way to breakfast. It's turned down to sixty degrees."

Bailey took over. "I think you should see the doctor."

Thelma turned from the stove and glared at Bailey. "I went to see Doc Stevens. If that woman was any more of a quack, she'd grow feathers and have webbed feet."

This harsh response took Fen aback. On any given day Thelma could argue with the sun about being late in rising or going down, but her assault on Dr. Stevens was too much. Something was definitely wrong.

Bailey threw caution to the wind and asked, "What did she say was wrong with you?"

"It's personal."

The room grew quiet for several seconds. Bailey seemed to collect her nerve and asked, "Is it serious?"

"The doc says it ain't, but what does she know?"

Fen put together the clues and eked out, "Ah-hah."

Bailey shifted her gaze to him. "What's wrong with her?"

Fen and Thelma stared at each other until he spoke. "You might as well tell her. She'll figure it out once she thinks about it."

Thelma put down the tongs. "That doc told me I'm going through the change. I'm too young for that foolishness. I'm getting a second opinion."

Fen stared at her but refrained from challenging her with words.

"Quit looking at me like that. I know Doc Stevens is right, but I don't have to like it."

"The change? You mean like menopause?" When no response came, Bailey asked, "How would you describe a hot flash?"

"It's like I've got the firebox from a locomotive in me and there's an ugly man shoveling in the coal."

"Yuk!"

"You said it, young lady. The Lord must have been extra mad at Eve to give us these flashes."

Smoke rose from the skillet. Thelma erupted in a blistering string of comments about burning the bacon. Fen motioned for Bailey to make a tactical withdrawal from the table.

Thelma was having none of it. "You two sit back down. You may not get bacon this morning, but you won't leave the table hungry. Bailey, get a cup of coffee and warm Fen's. He's only had two cups this morning."

Bailey filled their cups then joined Fen at the table. Her blue eyes sparkled with adventure. "Any idea what the crime is we're going to solve?"

"I'm not sure there is a crime. Chuck and Candy don't like to discuss business over the phone."

"Can I come with you?"

"It may have nothing to do with solving a case. There could be a dozen reasons for them calling."

"Good try, but we all know something's up. I want to go."

Fen considered her request. There was too much demand in her words, so he shook his head. "Part of maturing is developing the ability to practice patience. You stay here and work on the owl. If there's a case, I'll tell you about it when I get home."

"Bummer."

Thelma spoke as she dumped blackened bacon in the trash. "Not as big a bummer as mini-pause." She used the bottom of her apron as a makeshift fan. "Lord have mercy, somebody open the windows."

Chapter Two

Fen stabbed the first of three buttons mounted on the wall of his triple garage. Light dispelled darkness and a chain engaged overhead. Metal creaked as the garage door rose from its place of slumber. It wasn't long before the diesel engine in his one-ton pickup truck clattered to life, expressing its opinion of having to work on a frosty morning.

After clearing the posts of the warmish garage, Fen cut the wheels and pointed his truck to the gravel road that led to the entrance of his property. Sam appeared out of nowhere, standing by the driver's window. How the Choctaw Indian came and went with such stealth remained a mystery.

The engine's clatter muffled the sound of the window retreating into the truck's door. Sam frowned. "It's too loud. You should ride a horse or a bicycle."

"A horse or bicycle doesn't have a heater," said Fen. "Anything going on this morning?"

"Two new calves and your horse threw a shoe."

There was no need to ask Sam to call a farrier. The farm manager could re-shoe a horse as good as anyone in the county.

Fen also didn't need to ask if the heifers and calves were in good shape. If they weren't, Sam would have said so.

Sam asked, "How's Thelma?"

The question told Fen that Sam had slept someplace besides the cottage with his wife. This wasn't unusual, as he preferred to live outside regardless of the temperature.

"She's sweating and growling," said Fen in answer to Sam's question.

A slow nod came from Sam. "The doctor said it might take a week or two for the new medicine to work."

Thelma had not divulged this welcome piece of information, which didn't come as a complete surprise. She felt it was her duty to extract information from others, but sharing things about herself fell under the general heading of *none of your business*. Giving her opinions, however, flowed like the Brazos River that ran past Fen's four-thousand-acre property.

"You must be going to talk to your lawyer friend." Sam's comment was more a statement of fact than a question.

Fen confirmed Sam's words with a nod.

"That means you'll leave soon."

"It's possible. Bailey is itching to work another case."

A gust of wind sent a chill through Fen while Sam stood like a rock, unaffected by the elements. Fen asked, "Will it snow?"

Sam shook his head. "Sleet, but no snow. Clear by noon tomorrow." Sam walked away. He'd used his daily allotment of words.

By this time, the clattering of the engine wasn't as loud. It was like the truck had surrendered to its fate of not going back into the garage. Bailey and his truck had something in common. They performed well after they'd been up for a while. It was getting started on a chilly day that gave them trouble.

Fen slowly traveled the quarter of a mile to the front gate.

On the way, he viewed two oil storage tanks that were regularly serviced. The wells on his property served as one of his four continual sources of revenue. The first was a pension from the State of Texas for stopping a bullet with his knee when he served as a state trooper. That knee was now plastic and metal. Other income came from the sale of livestock and crops grown on the fertile land of the Brazos River bottom, and selling his paintings.

By the time the mechanical gate yawned open, his truck's heater was blowing warm air. He turned right onto a county road that led past Newman property, owned by his former father-in-law. Bad blood had existed between the two ever since Fen's wife died and Mr. Newman placed the blame on Fen for not insisting she pursue a second heart transplant. They'd reached a temporary truce, but there was no telling how long that would hold.

He removed his cowboy hat, ran the palm of his hand over freshly trimmed hair, and headed for the bridge over the muddy, rain-swollen Brazos River.

The trip into Springdale, the county seat of Newman County, went without incident. He soon eased his truck between the white lines of Chuck Forsythe's law office parking lot. The truck issued a quick toot of the horn as he pressed the key fob.

Candy, Chuck's wife, looked over her computer's monitor as he entered and greeted him with a warm smile. "The coffee's ready, and Chuck is in his office. I'll join you after I finish filling in the blanks on this contract."

Fen followed the smell of fresh-brewed Honduran coffee into the small kitchen. He retrieved his mug and filled it with what he believed to be the best cup of coffee in town. His boots made clomping sounds until he reached the carpet of Chuck's spacious office at the end of the hall. The door was open.

"You don't like people sneaking up on you," said Fen as he stopped at the portal.

Chuck looked up from a scrum of papers and files on his desk. It always seemed like the piles were competing for Chuck's attention. The attorney pointed to the chair on the opposite side of his desk.

"A good hardwood floor is less conspicuous than a bell on the door." He grinned. "In my profession, a little warning can help me head off trouble."

Fen looked in vain for a spot to rest his mug on the edge of Chuck's desk. None existed, so he rested it on his thigh, taking frequent sips until it cooled.

Candy breezed in, carrying yet another file, which she opened and handed to Chuck. "Sign here." She pointed to an underlined spot on the page.

He complied without hesitation, and she retrieved the file. She rounded the desk and settled into the chair next to Fen. "This shouldn't take long," she said.

"Is it another case?"

"Yes and no," said Chuck.

Fen shook his head. "That's an answer I'd expect from an attorney." He turned his gaze to Candy. "You speak Texan. Is it a case or not?"

She chuckled. "Let me explain. An elderly man named Gilbert Duvant died six months ago under unusual circumstances."

Chuck took over. "His home exploded." He threw his hands in the air. "Boom!"

"What kind of explosion?" asked Fen.

"The arson investigator said there was a propane build-up in the home that was set off by some sort of spark. The home was located a long way from the nearest volunteer fire department."

Candy added, "It was an old frame home that burned hot and long. The sheriff initially investigated the death as suspicious, but without evidence to prove otherwise, the case was officially ruled an accident."

Fen considered the words and what wasn't said. "Apparently, the ruling didn't satisfy everyone."

Chuck fiddled with a pen on his desk. "In his day, Gilbert Duvant was the top cattleman in Williamson County. He worked like a fiend and bought property in Williamson County when it used to be cheap. He was ahead of his time in that he raised prime beef for Austin's restaurants. His son, Gil, took over the ranch operation as soon as he left high school. He's the true entrepreneur in the family. Answers for his father's death are what Gil is demanding."

Fen shifted in his chair. "Something tells me he has enough pull with someone who can order an investigation that will look deeper into his father's death than the sheriff did."

The attorney's countenance didn't register an emotion, which came as no surprise. Shadowy, well-placed people around the state had formed an organization that looked into situations that fell through the cracks of law enforcement. Fen was content to act as a private investigator called upon a few times a year to help local and state police.

"How old was Mr. Duvant?" asked Fen.

Candy had the answer. "Ninety-four, but sharp of mind and still lived by himself."

Fen stayed silent until a question bubbled to the surface. "How much land are we talking about, and who did he leave it to?"

"About six thousand acres. Some of it is riverfront on the San Gabriel," said Chuck.

"Gilbert Junior was the sole beneficiary," said Candy. "He's in his seventies. Gil also has three sons, but they aren't named in the will."

Chuck chimed in, "If you're thinking the son might have killed his father, there's no motive. Gil's income is in the seven figures. He owns multiple prosperous businesses and knew his father's land was coming his way. All he had to do was wait."

Fen crossed his leg with the artificial knee over the other. "This sounds like pretty thin gravy. Is there a reason Gil thinks someone murdered his father?"

Chuck and Candy traded glances that seemed to ask, *Do you want to answer or should I?* Chuck asked, "Honey, do you know where I put the copy of the will?"

She stood and pointed to a stack of files. "Second folder down."

Chuck took the top file off the stack and placed it on another. He hinged the next file open and leaned back in his chair. "I'll skip down to the interesting part. Here it is: *I'm instructing my attorney to delay reading this for six months after my death. I want to give the police time to find whoever killed me.*"

Chuck closed the file and tossed it back onto a stack while Fen sat spellbound.

Fen murmured. "I'm not sure what to make of that. If his death was an accident, there's no crime, but..."

"Yeah," said Chuck. "But what if it wasn't an accident? That's why we want you to go to Georgetown and do a little digging."

Candy produced two pages with names, addresses, and phone numbers on it. She passed it to Fen. "Here's the contact information for everyone named in the will. I've also included the obituary the local newspaper published. These will give you a place to start."

"When was the will dated?"

Chuck fielded the question. "It was updated three months before Gilbert died. The only thing added was the delay to allow the police to investigate it as a murder."

Fen left the office more confused than when he arrived. Why would a man believe he would be killed? Could it be the imaginations of a man of advanced age? With no evidence that clearly pointed to a homicide, this could well prove to be an unsolvable case.

His thoughts settled on one thing that was firm ground. He'd never faced an investigation where he had to prove the commission of a crime before he could try to solve it. Not the easiest task to complete.

His mind jumped from one thing to the next. Should he take Bailey with him? On the one hand, she'd been working diligently and could use a brief road trip. On the other, she needed to stay focused on her art so she'd have an adequate supply of works to sell at the upcoming spring shows.

Thoughts shifted to the third member of his team. He spoke to himself as he drove. "What about Lou? Should I send her the list of names, or would that be wasting her time?"

He changed his mind several times on the drive back to his home.

Bailey must have been looking out the window of her studio, which was part of her apartment above the garage. She met him in the living room of the main house, where a fire crackled in the fireplace. Her face glowed with expectancy. "I packed for three days. Is that enough?"

"Too much," said Fen. "There may not be a crime to investigate."

Her countenance fell like a poorly constructed bridge. "That stinks." She paused. "Wait. Is there a crime or not?"

"Sit down and I'll tell you what I learned." Step by step, Fen walked her through the meeting he had with Chuck and

Candy. As was her habit, she interrupted frequently with questions. On the one hand, he welcomed the inquiries because it showed she had an agile, inquisitive mind. On the other hand, she lacked patience and tended to speak before she thought.

"Here's the bottom line," said Fen. "I'm going to Georgetown alone and talk to some of the family members. I'll also make an appointment with the sheriff."

Bailey interrupted. "What about Lou?"

"I'll send her the list of family members Candy gave me. Her skill is research. She might find something that would point to a motive, which could be useful."

Bailey pressed her lips together until they formed a thin line. "I still think I should go with you."

"I'm not saying no, only not yet. It won't be long before our spring shows start, and you need more works to sell. Also, I don't want you falling behind in your online college classes."

"Now you're making up excuses."

He sensed a crack in her resolve, so he kept talking. "Let's make a deal. If two of Gil Duvant's three sons believe their grandfather's death wasn't an accident, you can join me and we'll do a thorough investigation."

Bailey countered with, "One, not two, of the sons. That would mean two family members for and two against."

Fen shook his head. "All ties go to me. House rules."

"You made that up."

He responded with a smile.

Instead of exploding, she pursed her lips, stood, and walked away. Fen knew her to be both imaginative and cunning. She'd look for a way to turn the odds in her favor.

Chapter Three

The morning sun was two hours into its daily job of spreading light and warmth onto the flat farmland east of Taylor. The miles flew by and Fen's spirits rose with every mile that passed. He loved his home and its female occupants but had to admit that between Thelma's hot flashes and Bailey's cabin fever, the solitude of his truck's cab and a long drive were a welcome break. The singing of mud-gripping tires on asphalt was a tune he found both pleasing and refreshing.

Time to call Lou. He activated his phone clipped into a holder mounted on the dash. A groggy voice answered. "Yeah?"

"You're still in bed?"

"Call back in an hour and I'll tell you."

"I'll be in Georgetown in an hour."

"How long will it take you to get there?"

"Half an hour. Forty-five minutes at the most. I'm about twenty miles west of Taylor."

"Stop for donuts and coffee. You're an ex-cop. You should know where the donuts live."

Fen couldn't keep the corners of his mouth from lifting.

"That's a good idea. I'll call you back in twenty minutes. That will give you time to take your first dose of caffeine."

The phone call cut off without a salutation. He was confident that by the time he added a dessert to the breakfast Thelma had served him, Lou would be awake enough to talk.

Twenty minutes later, he brushed sugar from his lap, stepped from a small donut shop, and retrieved his phone from the pocket of a leather blazer. He climbed into the cab of his truck and told the phone to call Lou.

She answered on the fourth ring. "You sure know how to ruin a delightful dream."

"You were supposed to be sipping on caffeine to open your eyes."

"I made my double expresso and sat down to enjoy it, but fatigue won out before I took the first sip. It was a late night working on that list you gave me. That makes it your fault."

"Nothing new about that. Were you dreaming you received a Pulitzer Prize for literature?"

"Hardly. It involved a beach of white sand, an umbrella, and water as clear as the blue sky."

"No bronzed man with more muscles than brains?"

"Hardly. The men I attract fill only one of those criteria... no brains." She paused. "I don't hear your truck running. Are you still stuffing your face with fried bread drenched in sugar?"

Fen turned the key, and his truck came to life. "Is that better?"

"It's still too quiet. You're sitting still."

"Do you want me to call back when I'm past the city limits?"

"No, thanks. Now that I'm awake it's time to get to work."

With the obligatory banter out of the way, Fen followed Lou's hint and directed his attention to the reason for his trip. "What did you find out about Gilbert Duvant?"

"He was a workaholic, raised his own quality beef, invested in real estate, and raised a son who outperformed him."

"I already knew that. What about his mental state?"

"He was still active in civic organizations, an infrequent churchgoer, and lived alone without so much as a maid. In short, he was what they call a self-made millionaire. I know that's not a formal diagnosis, but he enjoyed good health and I couldn't find a whisper of mental health problems."

"Hmm," said Fen. It was a placeholder comment that meant nothing except to give him time to plan his next question. "That doesn't help much. I was sure you'd come up with some hint of senility or paranoia."

"Sorry to disappoint you. I might find something to contradict the published accounts if I had more time."

"Don't bother. What about Gil, his son?"

"I wish I was his fourth wife."

"Why?"

"I'd divorce him like I did the first three bums I married. At least with him, I'd get a decent settlement."

Fen had to backtrack and confirm something. "Did I hear you say he's been married three times?"

"Correct. Gil and I are both zero for three in choosing spouses. He had three sons by his first wife. Unlike him, I never had to change diapers. Thank goodness."

Fen passed the large grocery store on the north side of Taylor and increased speed. "What did you find out about the sons?"

"Not much. I didn't know if you wanted me to spend my time researching Gil's ex-wives or his sons."

"Let me think about that while you finish telling me about Gil."

The sound of Lou taking in a full breath came through the truck's speaker. "Gilbert Duvant, Junior. AKA Gil Duvant.

Age: seventy-two." She shifted her presentation to something that didn't sound like a criminal description of a suspect. "Gil has a true Midas touch with business. He more-or-less took over the ranch and cattle production from his father ten years after he graduated from high school. He was already investing in real estate. As a side note, Gil's eldest son, Chance, now runs the cattle operation."

"Uh-huh. Keep going."

"Gil and his father invested in property in and around Williamson County. One property is a restaurant that's a local landmark."

Lou kept on. "It was real estate that made the family big money. When I say Gilbert and Gil bought land, I mean big chunks of land in all the right places. No one could have guessed how much property would appreciate north of Austin back then. Gilbert and Gil worked like fiends, lived like paupers, and sunk all they could back into land. It was almost like they could smell the next big growth spurt and the businesses that would prosper."

Fen could see the success story unfold before him. Hard work, diverse skills, and timing combined to create a wealth-machine of extreme proportions. A question came to him. "Tell me about Gil's middle son."

"He lives in Georgetown and works for the city. That's all I have so far."

"What about the youngest son?"

"Robert Duvant didn't follow in the footsteps of his father or grandfather. He lives in Austin and is part of the music scene."

"That's a tough way to make a living. Is Robert estranged from the rest of the family?"

"I didn't get that far last night. Are you saying I'm to focus on the victim's grandsons?"

Fen rubbed his chin. Lou's question was one he'd expected but still wasn't sure how to answer. He took a stab in the dark and hoped he made the right decision. "Hold off on additional research. I have appointments with the sheriff and Gil today. I may want to stay another day or two and talk to Gil's sons who live in the county. If any of his former wives are still in the area, it may be worth talking to them, too."

Lou spoke with conviction. "You'd better find something juicy for me to write about. The most exciting thing I had to report on this week was that Norma Brown's cat pumped out six kittens and she had to rename Buddy to Belinda."

After the call ended, Fen chuckled to himself. "I guess Thelma was right when she said Norma's vision has been fading. Vanity can keep even an eighty year-old from seeing the optometrist."

He wound his way through the fertile river bottom and past numerous acres of fields with the first signs of green poking up through the rich, black soil. A voice on his phone told him to turn left in half a mile. Fen glanced at the truck's map outlining the directions to Gilbert Duvant's homestead and the enormous ranch. The sign on the bridge he approached read San Gabriel River.

No traffic appeared ahead or in his mirrors, so he slowed to inspect the river. It was a fraction of the Brazos that ran the length of his property, and the water was much clearer in the San Gabriel. To his left, he noticed a road that led to what looked like either the original bridge or a boat launch. He concluded a tiny boat, or more likely a kayak, would be all that could navigate the overgrown stream.

He'd trained himself to look for scenes to paint. There was something about old roads that disappeared into rivers or lakes that always caught his eye. They made him wonder what life was like on the old roads in days gone by. This might have been a shallow-water crossing that was impassable after heavy rains.

There was no rush to get to the sheriff's office, so he wheeled around and turned onto the road leading down to the river. Fen parked and took in the scene. He wondered about showing a horse-drawn wagon or a Model T Ford with water splashing from the wheels?

Several images came to mind of finished paintings from different angles. His hands formed a pretend, three-sided picture frame with his thumbs touching to form the bottom and his vertically extended fingers as the two sides. He telescoped out and back in by extending his arms or bringing them toward himself.

"Photos and a quick sketch," he said to himself. He pulled his phone from the pocket of his jacket and clicked a dozen shots at the angle he sensed the painting wanted. He might not admit it to any living person, but he believed his paintings spoke to him, only not with words.

With the phone back in his pocket, he retrieved an artist's pencil from his truck. Quick, sure strokes became images on his sketch pad.

Fen paid little attention to the vehicle that crunched over gravel as it approached and parked. He kept sketching until a man's voice said, "Good morning."

The greeting didn't scare him but took him away from what he called an artist's trance. That he'd slipped into it so quickly, verified the future painting was talking to him.

The man drove a pickup truck emblazoned with decals and lights that identified it as belonging to the Williamson County Sheriff's Department. As for the officer, he was on the young side. But perhaps that was a matter of his middle-aged perspective.

Fen dipped his hat as a greeting. "It's a nice day you

ordered. Not a cloud in the sky." He pushed his cowboy hat back on his head to give the officer a full view of his face. "I hope this isn't a private road. I didn't see a sign."

The officer shook his head. "No, sir. It's public. I've been parked on the side of the road watching you. Couldn't figure out what you were doing. Most people come here to launch a kayak, to fish, or explore the San Gabriel."

"I'm an artist. The old road looked like it wanted to be painted."

The officer chuckled. "That's not the first time I've heard an artist say that."

Fen stuck out his hand. "Fen Maguire."

Hands were shaking when the young man said, "Deputy Cory Blane. Nice to meet you, Mr. Maguire."

"Are you an artist?" asked Fen.

The young man had clear green eyes and gave a good, firm handshake. "Not me, but there's a bunch in town. In fact, I know a girl who painted this exact spot. She's darn good."

"Really? What's her name? I might know her."

"Ren Duvant. She's my age and lives in Georgetown."

This was more confirmation that he was in the right spot to paint. He looked to the west. "Is Ren part of the Duvant family that lost Gilbert Duvant a little over six months ago?"

Cory's eyes narrowed. "That's not common knowledge for someone who lives in Newman County."

Fen found the deputy's suspicious response amusing and aggravating at the same time. "That tells me you checked me out on your computer while I was sketching the river."

Cory took a step back. "I know your name, address, and that you have no outstanding tickets or warrants. What I'd like to know is what's under the camper shell of that fancy truck."

"Artist supplies and blank canvases."

"Mind if I search your truck?"

"I'll do you one better. Follow me to Sheriff Rhoads's office and you can search it while I'm meeting with Stony."

The deputy tilted his head and he squinted his eyes. "Who are you?"

"A medically retired highway patrolman and the former sheriff of Newman County."

With red creeping up the young man's neck, and no words coming forth, Fen took pity on him and changed the subject. He pointed to the west. "If I'm not mistaken, the land on the other side of that fence is Duvant land. Am I right?"

"Yes, sir. If you climb the riverbank, you can make out where the old man's house was on a hill. Ren told me he liked to look out over the river bottom and count his cattle."

After a final handshake, Fen got back on the road that would take him to Georgetown. He considered the conversation with Cory Blane. It had yielded him nothing in the way of fresh evidence. Perhaps Sheriff Rhoads would be of some help.

Chapter Four

Highway 29 led into Georgetown from the east. Fen usually approached the city on Interstate 35 if he was traveling from Austin to points north, like Waco or Dallas. A new, massive high school marked a boundary line of sorts, from mostly rural farmland to a city experiencing urban sprawl. What was once a sleepy bedroom community was showing all the signs of explosive growth. Apartments and new homes squatted on land previously occupied by crops and cattle.

He followed 29 past Southwestern University, a small enclave of higher education founded by Methodists. The ribbon of highway pointed due west and took him past renovated older homes of a bygone era. The maps program told him to turn right onto Austin Avenue. He wheeled the truck ninety degrees and headed north through the heart of Georgetown and past the regal county courthouse. Two blocks later, he turned left into a large parking lot. It overlooked the multi-story jail and the Monument Cafe.

Before climbing down from his truck, he sent a text to Sheriff Stony Rhoads announcing his arrival. They'd agreed to meet at the MONUMENT instead of the sheriff's office, which was conveniently located in the next block to the west.

With his Stetson securely anchored on his head, Fen strode into the art deco restaurant. It was the expanded version of the original MONUMENT CAFE, which had served the city faithfully for decades. This, however, was no small-town greasy spoon eatery. The owners prided themselves in serving farm-fresh ingredients prepared with exacting standards.

It wasn't long before the sheriff slid into the booth opposite him. Fen opened the conversation while scanning the restaurant. "This is quite the upgrade from the original one at the south end of Austin Avenue."

"Did you eat there when you were going through the highway patrol academy?"

Fen grinned. "We were suckers for the pies. It was like baiting the ground in front of a deer stand."

"Still is. The location changed and now they serve a lot of organically grown food. Otherwise, it's still one of the best restaurants around."

Fen took stock of Stony. He was a thick man with a chest like a rain barrel. There wasn't much neck showing over the collar of his shirt, and his hands looked wide and strong. If it weren't for the crisp uniform, he could be mistaken for a tradesman, one who spent his days laboring with pipes or concrete.

The server brought coffee. By some unspoken mutual agreement, they'd satisfied an unwritten rule of engaging in two minutes of inconsequential banter. Time to get down to business. Before either of them could start their conversation, a waft of perfume announced a woman stopping at the table.

"Good morning, Sheriff."

"It is indeed. Spring's right around the corner and I heard the lake calling my name on the way to work. Another week or two, and the fish will jump in the boat without me having to bait a hook."

Stony raised an open palm toward Fen. "Sunny, this is Fen Maguire. Fen, Ms. Sunny Day."

The introduction gave Fen the opportunity to inspect the woman. The word expensive came to mind. Whatever her age might be, which he guessed to be around thirty-five, she had the air of a sophisticated beauty with a hint of country cousin lurking in the background. He concluded she spent a lot of money on a personal trainer, a hair stylist, and designer clothes. Her posture was arrow-straight, yet she had a down-home charm about her that invited conversation.

"I like your name," said Fen. "It matches your face."

Sunny switched to a southern voice straight out of *Gone With the Wind*. "I do declare, Mr. Maguire, you make a girl blush. What brings a handsome man like you to our humble county?"

Fen used his cover story instead of giving the real reason. There was enough truth in it that his conscience wouldn't bother him. "I paint landscapes in oils, but lately I've been focused on Texas rivers. The San Gabriel interests me."

Stony cut into the conversation. "Fen's one of the best-known, most successful artists in the state."

The woman's accent switched back to her normal, pleasant voice. "How fascinating. Your wife must be extra special to have reeled you in."

Her words caught him off guard and momentarily speechless.

Stony quickly said, "Fen lost his wife a few years ago."

"Oh, dear," said Sunny. "I'm so sorry."

Fen issued an obligatory nod.

Stony took over the conversation, taking it out of the past

and into the future. "Sunny, you're dressed for business. I'm guessing you have another big client to sweep off their feet?"

She winked at Stony. "Not until this afternoon. I'm meeting Bart this morning to see what kind of bait he wants me to use to catch his next prey."

Stony shifted his gaze to Fen and explained. "Sunny is what you might call a deal facilitator. She identifies clients who are looking to move their businesses to the county. It's her job to point them to developers like Bart Hill. He's one of the county's big commercial and residential developers."

The break gave Fen time to find his words. "Your work must keep you busy."

"Not as busy as managing real estate." She glanced at the door. "There's Bart. I need to scoot. Nice to meet you, Fen."

"And you."

Fen caught only a glimpse of Bart Hill's back as he strode with purpose to a booth in another section of the restaurant.

"That woman's a perpetual motion machine," said Stony. "Always on the move and into something that makes money."

"Too fast for a country boy like me," said Fen.

"Don't let the look fool you," said Stony. "Sunny grew up poor and rough. She can drink fine wine or cheap whiskey. She'll transform herself into whatever she has to."

Fen stole a glance to where Sunny sat across the room. "Is Bart Hill the only person she works with?"

"No, but he's the biggest."

It was time to shift gears. Sunny was an interesting woman, but she wasn't the reason he was meeting with Stony. He looked across the table. "Did the reading of Gilbert Duvant's will make you have second thoughts about his death?"

"Of course it did. I had my top detective pull the file and go over all the evidence again with a fine-tooth comb. You know as well as I do how difficult it is to find evidence after a fire. There was no trace of accelerants. The fire was so hot that the body was nothing but a pile of ashes."

"Are you saying they couldn't positively identify the body?"

"The fire marshal said it was the hottest residential fire he'd ever seen."

Fen had his hands around the coffee cup like they needed warming. "What about threats against him?"

"None reported by any family members."

"What about someone after his land? I stopped at the old road by the river and again at the gate leading onto Duvant property. That's a big ranch."

Stony had his cup halfway to his mouth when Fen finished his question. The cup returned to the table. "Old man Duvant could have sold that land a hundred times over to any number of developers. They came out of the woodwork again after he died. Gil Duvant is so much like his father. He has no intention of selling family land. His home is on the property, and so is his eldest son's."

Fen took in the information and found it lacking in enough substance to justify an investigation. This left him with questions. "Do you have any explanation for why Gilbert Duvant thought someone would kill him, or why his son believes they did?"

Stony shook his head. "No to both questions. Gil might believe it, but his three sons don't."

"That surprises me. Why do you think none of them agree with their father?"

The sheriff's shoulders lifted and fell. "Perhaps it's because they're all set for life. Old man Gilbert's death doesn't affect them."

"Even the youngest?"

"That's Robert Duvant. He's doing that Austin-weird thing where he's happy as long as he can play music."

"I heard Gil and his son Robert don't get along. Do you think Gil will omit him from his will?"

"I spoke to Gil after the reading of his father's will. From what he said, all three of his sons will inherit plenty when Gil's gone. Believe me, there's enough to go around."

Fen stayed silent by taking sips of his coffee while the sheriff answered a text. One more question came to him as the sheriff put his phone back on the table. "Do you think it's a waste of time for me to pursue an investigation?"

"Yep, but I'll give you full access to everything I have. I've devoted all the time and resources I'm willing to spend without fresh evidence."

"You're probably right. After I speak with Gil and a few others, I'll take a day to decide."

"Good luck. Gil can be a tough man to say no to. He didn't get to be filthy rich by being timid."

Chapter Five

It was too pretty a day to stay inside, so Fen checked the maps program and located San Gabriel Park, a short drive from the cafe. He parked but continued to study the maps app on his phone. It showed the north and south branches of the San Gabriel River united in the park on its winding route through the county.

Recent moderate rains meant the two branches were flowing but came nowhere near testing the bank on the park side. The opposite shore was a high bluff of limestone rock. Fen wondered how many photos people had taken of the old concrete bridge that overlooked the peninsula where the waters of the San Gabriel joined. His thoughts shifted to his conversation with the sheriff. His head told him an investigation was a waste of time. Something deep within him, however, bothered him like an itch between his shoulder blades.

The river flowed by without a whisper of what to do. Perhaps a walk would help bring clarity. The first decision to make was whether to take a sidewalk toward the old bridge or walk along the river bank in the opposite direction. He chose the grass. It didn't take long before panhandling ducks begged for anything and everything. They quacked their disgust when he passed without responding to their pleas.

On he walked until he spotted a spring flowing from a rocky outcrop into the river. He bypassed it, only to discover a second spring. Walkers, bicyclists, and new mothers pushing strollers made for steady traffic on the path that meandered past playground equipment and multiple empty picnic tables. He walked almost a mile when he came to the sound of water tumbling over a stubby concrete dam.

On the way back to his truck, he noticed an abundance of squirrels whose homes were the massive pecan trees towering over the waterfront. It was a gorgeous park, but it held no answers to whether he should pursue an investigation.

His phone came alive as he approached his truck, causing another complaint from a duck with one of the ugliest faces he'd ever seen. He ignored the fowl and answered with a standard greeting.

"This is Gil Duvant. Where are you?"

"In San Gabriel Park."

"Where in the park?"

"In the parking lot near the old bridge where the two branches of the river come together."

"Stay there. I'm not far."

He looked at the phone after it cut off. "It seems Gil's a man of few words."

A shiny Chevy Silverado half-ton truck swung into a parking space one vehicle width away from Fen's truck. Out stepped a man wearing a western suit, polished boots, and a Silverbelly felt cowboy hat.

Fen righted himself from leaning on his truck.

"Sheriff Maguire?"

"It's just Fen Maguire."

A hand reached out for his. "Gil Duvant. You come highly recommended. Have you started your investigation yet?"

"I met with Sheriff Rhoads this morning. He's not convinced there's anything to investigate."

The muscles in Gil's cheeks flexed. "He's wrong, and I told him so. I hope his doubts haven't rubbed off on you."

Fen had seen this type of reaction before. He knew if he didn't say something to appease the gentleman rancher, this would be a short, unpleasant meeting.

"I'm here with an open mind. Why don't you tell me why you're convinced someone murdered your father?"

This seemed to mollify Gil enough to have a decent conversation. He looked at the cliffs on the far side of the river and then brought his gaze back to rest on Fen. "Did the sheriff tell you the reason they couldn't find any evidence?"

"It's my understanding the fire burned hot and long. It consumed any evidence that might have pointed to a murder."

Gil stuck his hands in his pockets. "Dad built that home after World War II." He shifted his gaze. "I should say he overbuilt it. Two-by-six walls on twelve-inch centers, not the standard sixteen inches. All prime lumber, siding, and knotty pine walls and cabinets. There was enough wood in that home to build two houses. The explosion blew out the windows, which sucked in air from all sides."

Fen nodded to keep him talking. "Do you believe the fire resulted from a propane leak?"

"I'm not questioning that, but it doesn't answer all my questions."

"Like what?"

"What caused the gas to form? Why didn't Dad or Billy smell it? They say Dad didn't wake up, but Billy would have."

Fen took a stab at a guess.

"Was Billy his dog?"

"Yeah, and propane gas smells like rotten eggs. There was nothing wrong with Dad's nose. Being a cop, you know about a dog's nose. One of them should have smelled it."

Fen nodded to encourage the flow.

"My father trained himself to be a light sleeper. Living in the country with coyotes looking for a meal of newborn calves made Dad a light sleeper."

Fen considered the patriarch's advanced age. Given that fact, he thought all of Gil's questions could have logical answers, but he backed away from pointing it out and asked, "Anything else?"

"The propane company was too quick to deny any responsibility."

"Are you suing them?"

"Not unless you can prove some sort of negligence." He huffed out a breath. "I think it's more likely someone tampered with one of the gas space heaters, which melted into puddles, even though they were mostly metal."

Gil's response showed Fen that the grieving son was capable of clear thinking. It would have been easy for him to blame the propane company or the heater manufacturer if he'd been after a fat insurance settlement.

"I already said this once, but I believe it's important enough to say again. Even if Dad had slept through the gas leak, Billy wouldn't have."

"Tell me about Billy."

"Dad's Australian Shepherd."

"Today's the first I've heard about Billy."

"He never left Dad's side unless he was working cattle."

Fen felt the scales tip slightly in favor of pursuing an investigation. An additional question came to him. "What did the investigators say about Billy?"

"They believed Billy was trying to get Dad up and out of the house when the explosion occurred."

"How old was he?"

"Thirteen. That's why the investigators and the sheriff quit investigating a long time ago. That breed's normal lifespan is ten to twelve years. They don't understand what good shape both of them were in."

The scales tipped back to the neutral position and even swung the other direction. A geriatric man, an old dog, a brokenhearted son, but no physical evidence weren't enough to convince him to spend much more time in Georgetown.

He looked to the river for advice, then remembered words his wife had given him. "When in doubt, delay and pray." The next thing that came to his mind was the MONUMENT's signature chocolate pie. He wouldn't mind spending a little more time here just to see if it's as good as he remembered.

Fen pulled in his thoughts like they were attached to a rope. "On the outside chance that I'm wrong, I'd like to go to your ranch and look at where your father's home stood."

"There's nothing left but a chimney, but you're welcome to kick around if you think it will do any good. The gate stays open during daylight."

Fen paused long enough to take in a full breath. "It wouldn't be right for me to build false hope. As things stand now, there's not a thimbleful of evidence to suggest someone murdered your father. I'll find a hotel room, spend the night, and go over the evidence and statements."

A dark cloud came over Gil's countenance. "Why bother? You've ignored everything I just said about Dad and Billy. You and Sheriff Rhoads must be twins."

It didn't take a genius to realize Gil's words were spoken from a position of anger and grief.

Fen lowered the volume of his reply. He was determined

not to get into a verbal brawl with Gil. "One night in town and a review of the sheriff's file is the most I can commit to. I'll call you tomorrow morning."

Gil ran his tongue over his top teeth like there was a foul taste in his mouth. "They told me you were a decisive man who got things done. It seems they were wrong."

There was enough truth and venom in Gil's words to cause Fen to clamp his teeth together. The words stung, but they also revealed a side of Gil's personality that he'd hidden up to this point. The new patriarch of the Duvant empire wanted his desires met without delay.

As the millionaire's truck sped away, Fen wondered if Gilbert Sr.'s temper rivaled that of his son. If so, his son orchestrating the death of his father after an argument would certainly be a possibility.

That sounded too Shakespearian, but Fen knew the acquisition of wealth, power, and positions of prestige was as powerful as any narcotic. Was Gil tired of his father having the title of patriarch? Unlikely, but not impossible. Perhaps the fire wasn't a tragic accident.

The San Gabriel carried a bottle downstream at a leisurely pace. Fen climbed into the cab of his truck. He wondered how long it would take the bottle to pass by the Duvant ranch. Hours? Days? He'd most likely be long gone by then. Or would he?

Chapter Six

The gate of the Duvant ranch was open just like Gil said it would be. Fen remembered the words of Deputy Cory Blane and followed a gravel road to a hill overlooking the river bottom. A soot-stained chimney told him he was standing in front of all that remained of a couple's dream home. Children had once played on the spot he stood, and the fertile land behind him yielded enough to start a family empire.

Fen turned and scanned the ribbon of water that set a boundary to the land. He considered painting what lay before him, knowing it would sell. There was always a market for picturesque river valleys.

His thoughts returned to the purpose of his visit to the ranch. After six months, the land was well on its way to reclaiming the spot where Gilbert Duvant had toiled to build his home.

An amble around the perimeter of the charred area revealed what Fen expected... nothing. He continued on to what once was the backyard. Pecan and peach trees dotted the area. They'd provided food as well as shade from the blazing

Texas sun. The absence of trees in front of the home left an unobstructed view of the river valley from what had probably been an east-facing front porch.

A derelict garden plot occupied much of the backyard. Fen wondered how many volunteer plants might spring up in the coming months. The remnants of a fence wouldn't keep out any of the animals that would appreciate an unexpected snack of squash or tomatoes.

The day was moving toward the noon hour, but Fen was in no hurry, so he snapped photos taken from the front and side yards. His artist's muse invited him to tarry and make a sketch of what lay before him. He retrieved an easel, his large sketch pad, and pencils. Perhaps the ashes of the home would release its secrets to him. He wondered out loud, "Was someone responsible for what happened to Gilbert? Gil believes they were, but I'm not so sure."

Fen continued to ask questions but it seemed the remnants of the home had instructions to remain silent. This didn't bother Fen as he'd grown accustomed to hours alone and to the sound of his own voice. Silence in response to his questions was normal.

The distant rumble and rattle of an approaching vehicle caught Fen's ear. It was an ATV similar in style to the one used on his ranch. The driver looked to be in his late forties, with sprigs of gray showing from under a dirty, felt cowboy hat. He wore the obligatory attire of a rancher: boots, blue jeans, a long sleeve shirt, and a vest.

What Fen wasn't expecting to see was an empty holster on the man's hip. It was empty because the man held a Model 19, forty-five-caliber pistol. The business end was aimed at Fen's chest.

"Step back and keep your hands where I can see them," said the rancher.

It wasn't the first time Fen had looked down the barrel of a pistol, but he never liked the experience. He took a step back and two to the side with hands raised to shoulder height. "This pencil contains lead but it isn't loaded with bullets."

"Funny. Keep your hands up until deputies get here and take you to jail. Didn't you see the *no trespassing* sign at the front gate?"

"If you're Chance Duvant, I met with your father this morning and he gave me permission to come here."

"You may know my name, but my father put me in charge of this property and what I say goes."

The sound of an approaching siren caught on the northwest breeze. Fen wanted to test Chance. "It will take that deputy a good three minutes to get here. I'm going to unzip my jacket with my left hand, lift it up, slowly turn around, and show you I'm not armed."

"If you do, I'll put a slug in the middle of your belly."

"I don't think you're that stupid. I have permission from the landowner to be here. You have too much to lose by shooting an unarmed man."

Fen took in a shallow breath and hoped he hadn't misjudged the man. "I'll be putting my right hand higher and using only my left hand to unzip."

It might as well have been a slow-motion film. Fen did as he said he would. A bead of sweat slid between his shoulder blades. "Satisfied?"

Trying to save face, Chance said, "You're lucky I'm in a good mood."

Fen lowered his hands. If Chance was going to shoot him, he'd have already done so.

"Who are you?"

"The name's Fen Maguire. Your father wants me to investigate the death of your grandfather."

"Waste of time," said Chance as the sheriff's office truck charged up the hill and slid to a stop.

Out jumped Cory Blane. "What's going on, Mr. Duvant?" He took a double take when he saw Fen. "Hello again, Sheriff Maguire."

Chance spoke as he tried to holster his pistol, but missed at the first attempt. "Sheriff?"

"Used to be," said Fen. "Now it's an honorary title."

Cory interrupted. "I spoke with Sheriff Maguire this morning. He's a former state trooper and sheriff. Now, he's a famous artist. I need to tell dispatch there's nothing wrong." He paused. "There isn't anything wrong, is there?"

Chance answered with a weak "No." It was enough for Cory. He retreated to his truck.

Slow steps took Chance to where he could see Fen's sketch of the river valley. "Dang. That's good. Cory wasn't kidding when he said you're an artist."

"Thanks."

"Sorry I pulled my gun on you."

"I appreciate you not shooting me."

Cory had returned and was ready to join the conversation. "It wouldn't be the first time somebody shot him. That was when he was a highway patrolman."

Fen reached down and tapped his right kneecap. "I finally broke down and got an artificial knee last summer. I'm not a good patient and hated the thought of a doctor cutting on me." He cut his gaze to look full at Cory. "Did you spend the morning doing a computer search on me?"

He nodded. "That and patrolled. It doesn't take long to give out a couple of tickets. I had plenty of time to do a search. Tell me about that cute girl artist you're training."

"Bailey showed up when you searched for me?"

"Not exactly. I had to follow a thread. Is it true she's already helped you solve two murders?"

"Four. The most recent was in Wichita Falls."

"Four? I've been a deputy for a year and a half and haven't been involved in a murder yet."

Chance made his presence known. "It's a good thing there's no murder to investigate here."

"That's not what your father says," said Cory.

This was a favorable turn of events. Cory had stated exactly what was on Fen's mind.

Chance directed his words to Cory. "My father is chasing shadows. He believes someone is after him, too."

"Who?" asked Cory.

Chance hooked his thumbs in his gun belt. "Shadows are like apparitions and ghosts. They don't have names because they don't exist. You didn't get to know Granddad, but he was the most superstitious old cuss in the county. He passed it on to Dad like it was a genetically dominant trait."

Cory challenged him. "Does that explain your dad being run off the road at the big curve going to town?"

Fen wanted to ask when that happened, but Chance spoke before he could. With index finger pointing at Cory, Chance exclaimed. "A foggy morning, slick asphalt, too much speed, and being too cheap to keep decent tires on his truck explains that."

Cory shook his head. "Your dad swears a box truck forced him off the road."

"My dad also consulted a medium to tell him if he should marry his second wife. That one lasted a little over a year and cost him 1.2 million dollars."

Fen schooled his features to cover his surprise. Lou indicated Gil's ex-wives received generous compensation, but he wasn't expecting it to be that generous. Could an ex-wife, or even a future ex, have had something to do with Gilbert's death? How much money had Gil paid out to former wives over the years?

Lost in thought, Fen missed the question posed to him by Chance. "What's that?" he asked.

"Are you going to stay here much longer? I don't mind if you do, but close and lock the gate if you stay until dark."

Fen looked toward the river. "If you don't mind, I'd like to stay another hour or two. I do some of my best thinking when I'm out in nature, looking at a river."

Cory extended a hand for Fen to shake. "Good to see you again, Sheriff Maguire. I don't know if I'm supposed to say I hope you and Bailey work this case or not."

"Like I said," said Chance. "There's nothing to work."

"You're probably right, Mr. Duvant," said Cory. "My interest is selfish. I'd like to meet that Bailey girl and ask her what it's like to help investigate a murder. I hope for your family's sake I'm not standing on a crime scene."

Cory's truck and Chance's ATV pulled away in a much more sedate manner than they'd arrived. Fen settled into the silence and put light marks on the paper. He had a decision to make. The news that Gil believed someone tried to run him off the road inclined Fen to pursue the investigation. That Chance had a logical explanation tilted his thinking in the opposite direction again.

While looking at the sketch, he reached into his pocket for a coin to flip. He withdrew an empty hand. He'd need to keep searching for an answer.

Two hours passed as Fen allowed his thoughts to wander wherever they wanted. He found this emptying of his mind therapeutic, with the added benefit of the occasional revelation. The ringing of his cell phone spoiled the tranquility and put a squirrel to flight up a pecan tree.

Bailey's name appeared on the screen. Her mouth engaged as soon as he answered. "I've got it!"

"Got what?"

"The answer to the question."

She was spraying her words so fast he was having a hard time understanding her.

"Slow down. I was sketching and had my mind in neutral. What question?"

A huff sounded. "You need to listen faster. We're taking the case. Lou and I are coming to Georgetown."

"Before you pack, you'd better tell me what Lou discovered."

The rate of her speech and the volume increased. "You never give me credit for helping. You always assume Lou does all the work."

Fen jumped in. "Just tell me what you found."

This time, she shouted. "Another family member who believes someone killed Gilbert Duvant."

"One of his three grandsons? I know it's not Chance. I've already interviewed him."

"No. Listen, will you? It's his great-granddaughter, Ren Duvant."

Fen's mind flew back to the conversation he'd had with Cory that morning. "I heard something about Ren this morning. How would she know anything about her great-grandfather's death?"

"That doesn't matter. You told me if I could find one more family member who believed his death wasn't an accident, we'd investigate. I'm holding you to our agreement. Lou doesn't want to come until tomorrow, but I can come tonight."

"Pump the brakes and slow down. Who's Ren's father?"

"Robert Duvant."

"The musician?"

"So?" she demanded. "We're artists."

Fen shook his head as he spoke. "Are you letting your desire to get away from Thelma cloud your judgment?"

"You didn't waste any time leaving this morning, and you set the rules of what had to happen for us to take the case."

He had to admit that she'd made two good points. Bailey functioned best when she had specific tasks to complete, ones that gave her a sense of accomplishment. "Wait until tomorrow afternoon to come. Bring paint supplies and clothes for three days. If we need to stay longer, one of us can travel home and back in half a day."

An idea jumped into his mind. "Get on your computer and find a three-bedroom Airbnb for a few days. I'll stay in a hotel tonight. If we're going to do this, I need to go by the sheriff's office and get the case files of Gilbert Duvant's death."

"I'm on it. What else?"

"You must have talked to Ren Duvant today."

"Sure did. She paints murals on buildings. Isn't that cool?"

"Yeah. I'll want a full report on her and why she thinks someone killed her great-grandpa."

"Got it. What else?"

"Call Lou and tell her full background checks on all family, including Gil Duvant's three ex-wives and any children or grandchildren."

"She's already working on it."

Fen was silent for a minute. "That means you called her after you talked to Ren and before you called me."

He was winding up to give her an adult-sized chewing out when she said, "Things to do. I'll send you a text and let you know where we're staying while we work on the case."

The line went dead. It took him a while to get past the anger, but when he did, he smiled. They might not solve the case, but at least he had his answer as to whether they'd try. It came in an unorthodox manner but there was no going back.

He looked upward at the wispy clouds. "Happy, Sally?"

A pecan fell from an overhanging limb and hit the leg of his easel. He looked at the bare branches of the tree. Not another pecan in sight.

Chapter Seven

Steam rose from Fen's coffee cup that sat on the nightstand next to his bed at Georgetown's Hilton Hotel. He'd splurged on a room with a glimpse of the north branch of the San Gabriel. Copied files related to the fire and death of Gilbert Duvant sat on the bed next to him. It wasn't a completely sleepless night, but he felt the effects of poring over the investigator's findings until after midnight. Nothing that coffee wouldn't cure.

A framed photo of Sally sat on the room's desk, facing him. He slipped into sweat pants, pulled on his jacket, and adjusted the thermostat on his way to what he considered his most important meeting of the day. Three steps toward the desk and he had to retreat to grab his coffee. The executive chair greeted him with only a small squeak of complaint.

"Good morning, honey."

No response, but he wasn't expecting one. It helped ground his day to continue their long-held habit of starting their day together. He leaned back, took a sip of stimulant, and launched into a recounting of yesterday's events. Once finished, he asked her what she thought his chances were of finding out if someone murdered Gilbert. He played advocate for the opposition and said, "I think this will be a waste of time."

Sally offered nothing to his comment other than the same knowing smile he'd studied for years.

Fen kept talking. "I spent most of the night reading and making notes. Nothing much stood out. Yesterday was a bust, too. Are you sure I'm supposed to keep at it?"

This time, a nut didn't fall from an otherwise fruitless tree. He was on his own to decide how to proceed. He picked up the framed photo and looked at the face that still made his heart flutter. "Without evidence, I'm relying on intuition and hunches. That's no way to solve a case, and you know it."

He summarized what he'd found in the files so he wouldn't bore both of them. He sensed she appreciated his brevity, and he certainly did.

Time rarely had meaning when he spoke with Sally and today was no exception. He had until eleven that morning to check out of the hotel. After showering, shaving, and dressing for the day, he stuffed some of his items into a piece of carry-on luggage.

The ringing of his phone delayed his departure and a search for breakfast. The caller ID shone with Bailey's name.

Fen cleared his throat. "Good morning. How are things at the ranch?"

"It's in my rearview mirror. Thelma's miracle pills haven't kicked in yet. I had to get out of there."

Fen couldn't blame her for escaping. Instead of commenting on Thelma's personality quirks and hormone issues, he landed on a topic that was less confrontational. "What time can we check into the home you found?"

"Not before three o'clock." She gulped a breath. "I know what you're going to say, so don't bother. You don't have to worry about me hanging around all day being bored. I have plans to meet with Ren and get to know her. I'm going to sketch while she paints. We're meeting at a coffee shop in George-town. She can't wait to meet you."

"I'm looking forward to meeting her and asking why she believes someone killed her great-grandfather. She could be an unexpected gold mine of information. Make sure you don't press her too hard or fast. Establish rapport and allow her plenty of time to respond. Call me if you have any trouble."

Fen regretted what he'd said the second it passed his lips.

The huff of disgust blew like a cold gale out of his phone. She followed it with, "Do you have any idea how old you sound? In case you haven't noticed, I'm not six years old."

He had to admit that Bailey was old beyond her years. Her widowed mother all but abandoned her during her formative years, leaving the child to raise herself on the streets of Hous-ton. Street smarts she had. Interview experience was still a work in progress.

Bailey had more to say. "If you insist on keeping tabs on me, Ren wants to show me the murals she's painted on buildings around town. After that, we're grabbing a sandwich to go and heading out to her grandfather's ranch."

"I went there yesterday. If you're hoping to find clues in the ashes, don't bother."

Another huff, but this one communicated impatience more than disgust. Eye rolls, tone of voice, posture, and gestures were her preferred method of communication in person. On the phone, she had to use a mix of words and guttural utterances.

The pace of her words slowed, like she was the adult and he was the child. "I told Ren I wanted to paint the San Gabriel. She told me the old road you went to by the bridge is where everyone goes. Better spots are downstream, but you can only access them from her grandfather's land. That's where we'll be this afternoon." She let out a huff. "Was that slow enough for you?"

Fen responded with, "Oh." It was a two-letter response that communicated Bailey was two steps ahead of him. He retreated before she turned the tables on him and asked for his plans to further the investigation today.

Having made none, he changed the subject. "Do you know when Lou's leaving town?"

"Not until tonight. The editor wants her to get ahead on articles for the local newspaper. She's convinced the trip to Georgetown is a waste of her time."

"I'm thinking the same thing."

"No way. You'll both think differently after you talk to Ren."

Fen considered asking Bailey why she was so sure but refrained from starting that conversation. Feelings and hunches sometimes meant more to her than evidence. He had to admit that he was guilty of the same at times.

A plan for the day's activities leaped into his mind. "I spent the night reviewing the sheriff's files on the fire. When you pass over the San Gabriel east of Georgetown, look to your left. I'll be down there putting pencil to canvas."

"I told you that spot is where everyone paints and takes photos. Weren't you listening?"

"Think sales and marketing. There are reasons everyone chooses that spot. How many artists have painted the Eiffel Tower or the Grand Canyon?"

"You're probably right, but I'm going for something wild and unique."

"Knock yourself out. You might find a spot that will set the standard for Texas river scenes."

"I'll settle for wild, unique, and good enough to sell for a truck payment."

The call ended and Fen gathered his belongings. Some of Bailey's enthusiasm had transferred to him, both for the investigation and painting. The two artists had a symbiotic relationship. Losing himself in applying paint to canvas helped him to think and tap into the shadowy world of creativity. The mental rigors of gathering evidence and interviewing suspects forced him to use the other side of his brain, the one that favored science and unyielding logic. They both could ignore meals if their muse or a deadline pressed them to paint without breaks.

Bailey's idea of picking up a sandwich and going somewhere remote to paint appealed to him. A convenience store on his way out of town provided all his basic needs: a large cup of coffee, two bottles of water, breakfast tacos, and a turkey and cheese sandwich for lunch. He also threw in a pack of cookies at the checkout.

His next stop was at the makeshift parking lot overlooking the old road that dipped into the San Gabriel. He'd paint a side angle of the road, looking downstream. Minutes melted into hours as he began a well-rehearsed process of starting with faint marks from a hard-lead pencil. He established a horizon line that divided the earth from the sky.

The river was in no hurry, nor was he to make outlines on the canvas. Now and then he'd place a sketch pad in front of the canvas and draw something with an odd angle or unusual shape. Over the years, he'd learned the importance of details. Best to slow down and get them right with pencil instead of unforgiving oils.

The ringing of his phone broke his concentration. It came as a surprise to see the time read four fifteen. The days grew wings when he painted. Bailey's name shone on the screen. He opened his mouth to offer a greeting but only said, "Hey," before a distress-laden voice interrupted.

"Come here! There's a hand sticking out of the ground."

Chapter Eight

Bailey's announcement of a gruesome scene struck Fen dumb for several seconds. He shifted into cop mode. "Take your time and tell me where you are."

"Next door! I mean, on the other side of the fence from you." She gasped for breath. "I'm on the Duvant ranch, near the river."

"Slow down. Take in a deep breath and let it out slowly. Then tell me exactly where you are."

The sound of Bailey inhaling and slowly exhaling came through the phone's speaker. "We're about three-quarters of a mile downstream from where you are. You'll see my truck."

"Are you sure it's a human hand?"

"It sure looks like one. Nothing but bones. There's a hand with two fingers missing and about three inches of the two bones in the lower arm."

Fen pictured the scene. His mind went to Gilbert Duvant. Was it possible he didn't die in the house fire? If so, whose ashes had they found?

Just as fast, his focus went back to Bailey. "Don't touch anything. Does it look like it could be a grave?"

"Yeah. It's close to a stream that flows into the river."

"Back away from it. How close is your truck?"

"About thirty yards."

"Go to it. Have you called anyone else?"

"I haven't. Ren's calling her Uncle Chance."

Fen considered the best course of action. "You and Ren sit in your truck and wait for Chance. Let him make the call to the sheriff's department."

"Why not me or Ren?"

"I'll explain later."

"Are you coming?"

"Not until after the first cop arrives and secures the crime scene. I'll pack and listen for sirens."

Bailey had recovered enough to challenge him with a question, which was a good sign. "Why don't you want to look for clues before the cops arrive? That's what detectives do in the movies."

"I'll explain tonight after the police finish questioning you, Ren, and Chance. Plan on a late supper."

Fen pressed the phone closer to his ear as Bailey spoke to Ren. "Fen says for us to sit in my truck and not touch anything."

A distant voice said, "Uncle Chance told me to do the same thing. It must be an old-guy way of dealing with death."

Bailey responded with, "Fen knows what he's talking about. Let's get to the truck."

"What about our easels and sketch pads?"

Fen shouted, "Leave them!"

"He says to leave them. It's a crime scene."

Bailey's voice sounded louder, more in control of her emotions. He could tell she was now talking to him. "We're walking back to the truck. I see Chance's truck barreling this way. He's still a long way off."

"I hear him but can't see him. Stay in the truck until the police tell you to get out. Have your driver's license handy and give clear, concise answers to their questions. Don't volunteer answers to questions they don't ask. Watch out for open-ended questions. Don't guess. When in doubt, tell them you don't know."

"This won't be the first time I've spoken to cops. I know they're looking for suspects."

He held the phone away from his ear and disconnected the call. Without a hesitation he told it to call Sheriff Rhoads.

"Fen. I didn't expect to hear from you so soon."

"I wanted to give you a heads up. It seems my artist protégé, Bailey Madison, and Ren Duvant are on Gil's ranch. They believe they found the remains of a body near a creek that flows into the river. Chance Duvant is on his way to them. I told Bailey to let him look and call it in."

"Are they sure it's a human hand?"

"I don't know about Ren, but Bailey's used to painting details, and she's not squeamish. She said it's a human hand with two fingers missing. Expect a call from Chance in a few minutes."

"I'll get deputies headed in that direction. Do you know exactly where they are?"

"Close to the river, about three-quarters of a mile downstream from the bridge. How 'bout I meet you at the gate?"

"I'm walking out of my office now. Park on the ranch side of the cattle guard."

Fen's second phone call went to Lou. Highway noise accompanied her strained greeting. "Any good stories you'd like to tell me about?"

"Do you have your camera?"

"That's a foolish question to ask a reporter. There's one on my phone and one in my overnight bag. Do I need it?"

"Bailey found what she thinks is a human hand sticking out of the ground on the Duvant ranch. How long before you can get here?"

"Thirty minutes doing the limit. Twenty if you pay the ticket."

"Put the hammer down when you get past Taylor. Deputies and state troopers will be busy."

Late afternoon meant an increase in traffic on Highway 29. Steady, but not so much that he had trouble making the trip west to the entrance of the Duvant ranch.

Fen waited until a sheriff's department pickup truck came past with siren screaming and emergency lights ablaze. It wasn't long before a highway patrol SUV sped past with equal urgency. It was time for him to get to the ranch and wait for Sheriff Rhoads.

Fen made it onto Duvant property and pulled well off the road. Two more sheriff's department SUVs zipped past him. He'd timed it well as the sheriff pulled beside him before he could finish his pack of cookies. The sandwich remained in the sack, uneaten.

Crumbs fell from Fen's jacket as he exited his truck. The grim face of the sheriff matched his words as Fen climbed in beside the sheriff and latched his seat belt. "It's a human body, all right."

Fen's Stetson dipped and returned.

The sheriff kept both hands on the wheel as they left the gravel road and bounced along the fence line. "If this proves to be old man Duvant there's going to be egg on a bunch of faces, and one of them is mine."

Fen stated the obvious. "There'll be plenty of blame to go around. Forensics must have missed something." Fen remembered a detail he'd read in their report. "Didn't their analysis show human ashes in the living room?"

Stony responded with, "Uh-huh. It did. That's what convinced me Gilbert Senior perished in the fire."

A deputy stretched crime scene tape on the far side of a creek bed as they came to a stop alongside a state trooper's vehicle. A man wearing the khaki uniform of a highway patrolman stood at the edge of the dip in the earth, along with a second deputy sheriff, this one a female.

The state trooper and the deputy turned and strode toward Fen and Stony. "It's a human hand and lower arm," said the woman. "The thumb and index finger are missing, but there's a wedding band and some material on the arm."

"Call forensics," said Stony as he turned to glance at the grave. "Were you first on scene?"

"Second. Cory Blane is taping off the area."

"Help him after you call forensics. I'll get someone posted at the front gate. I don't want any nosy reporters flying in here. Where's Chance Duvant?"

The deputy pointed. "In the back seat of that truck with two young women." She unclipped a driver's license from under a pen in the pocket of her vest. "I know Chance and Ren Duvant, but this girl is from Newman County. She claims to be an artist who lives with the former sheriff who's now some hotshot artist and private investigator. I don't believe her. I haven't searched her for drugs yet, but I'll bet anything she's on something. Even if she isn't, she's hiding something."

Fen couldn't suppress the chuckle that bubbled out of him.

Stony pointed to Fen. "This is former sheriff Fen Maguire. The girl is who and what she claims to be." He took in a quick breath and added. "As for him being a famous artist, let's just say you'd need to save up for about a year to afford one of his smaller works."

A delicate shade of pink rose into the deputy's neck, up to her chin. "Sorry, Sheriff Maguire."

"No need to apologize. I told Bailey to make her words few. That doesn't come naturally to her. I'm not surprised you thought she was hiding something."

Stony wasn't so forgiving. "Instead of helping Cory tape off the area, go to the front gate. If they don't have a badge, don't let them get past you."

Fen needed to get Lou close without rupturing his relationship with Stony. He had an idea but wasn't sure Lou would like it.

A sheriff's department captain and a highway patrol sergeant arrived in close succession. Stony walked over to his captain and had a private conversation. The highway patrol sergeant joined Fen and the state trooper.

It had been almost thirteen years since Fen patrolled the highways and county roads, mainly around Newman County, but he was familiar with Williamson County. He didn't know the sergeant, but the lawman knew of Fen. The three discussed the scene and waited for the sheriff to return.

Stony pulled Fen aside. "I'd like your advice. Even if my forensic team did everything by the book, they're going to take heat if that body belongs to Gilbert Duvant. What do you think I should do?"

Fen rubbed his chin as he considered the question, which was political, not procedural. The sheriff was in damage control mode. An opponent could roast Stony in the next election for mistakes made by his forensic team. Their inability to identify the remains of a leading citizen and the patriarch of the Duvant clan spelled trouble.

"You're not coming out of this without a bloody nose," said Fen. "If it were me, I'd call the Texas Rangers and have them send in the state's forensic team."

The sheriff issued a reluctant nod. "That takes care of processing the crime scene. What about the investigation?"

"Do you trust your detectives to do a thorough job?"

"Well..." He squared his shoulders. "They're well educated and thoroughly trained, but their investigation came to a quick halt when forensics found human ashes. To be perfectly honest, my top detective isn't as motivated or thorough as he once was."

"Then let them prove themselves and make you the hero."

Stony was quick to add, "If the state crew identifies the body as belonging to Gilbert, certain people will be after my scalp."

"Which makes it even more important to get ahead of the story." Fen added. "Light a fire under your detectives and turn them loose on this. You'll know by tomorrow if it's Gilbert."

"How can you be so sure?"

"There'll be another set of bones in the same grave."

"Whose?"

"Billy. Gilbert's dog."

"I'd forgotten about Billy."

Fen realized Stony hadn't shifted from thinking like a politician when he said, "I can see another potential problem."

"What's that?"

The sheriff pointed an index finger at Fen. "You."

"Me? Why am I a problem?"

"If the Austin press catches wind that a private investigator was working on the case before my team, they'll roast me alive."

Fen knew Stony was right. He also knew Lou was barreling toward them with two cameras, a recorder, and press credentials ready to flash. She wouldn't take no for gathering a story, even if it meant wading down the river or launching the drone she kept in her trunk.

"I have a solution, but you probably won't like it," said Fen.

Chapter Nine

The old feeling of over-promising and under-performing washed over him, but he didn't see another way out. Lou didn't mind making people uncomfortable by writing the truth. It was as easy as breathing to her. She and the sheriff were on a collision course, and it was up to Fen to keep them from smacking into each other, or at least minimize the crash. He also hoped his plan would help the sheriff out of the mess he found himself in.

"Stony," said Fen. "It's been my experience that every time I tried to cover up a mistake, it came back to bite me. Know what I mean?"

The sheriff gave him a distrustful stare. "What are you trying to say?"

"I'm talking about reporters. Do you know I work with one? She was a top reporter in Dallas. Her name is Lou Cooper. She's already done a lot of background information on the Duvant family members for me. What she has might save your detectives some time."

The sheriff shook his head. "If you're trying to make a deal,

I'm not having a reporter at this crime scene. It's far enough away from the road on private property that I can get Chance and his father to insist I enforce the no trespassing signs at the gate."

"I know you can, but that won't stop her."

"Sure it will. My officer will arrest her as soon as she refuses to leave."

Fen pointed to the river. "Lou's headstrong as they come. She'll walk through the water in the river to get a photo of the crime scene. The river doesn't belong to anyone."

Stony ground his teeth.

The sheriff needed a lifeline, and Fen threw it at him. "I have an arrangement with Lou. She'll bend the story a little if it harms the investigation. I'll tell her she needs to show you and the sheriff's department in the best possible light."

Stony resettled his hat on his head. "I don't like it."

"I don't expect you to, but it's the lesser of two evils."

The sheriff narrowed his gaze. "What aren't you telling me?"

Fen had to come clean. "Lou's initial stories are for television and newspapers. They portray the police in a favorable slant. Way in the future, she'll publish a book, or books, that will go into detail and be her version of what happened. Those books are her retirement plan."

"When will she publish them?"

"By that time, you'll be retired and my teeth will be in a cup by my bed."

This earned a tense smile. "Not a pleasant mental image or much of a bargain."

"Neither is getting cooked over a fiery flame by big-city reporters looking to make a name for themselves."

Hesitation filled the sheriff's voice. "Are you sure she's not a cannibal waiting for me to be served at a barbecue?"

"She has a mind of her own, but she's fair, and she needs more stories."

The sheriff looked toward the river. "I can't stop her from walking down the river. If I keep her on this side of the tape, at least she can't get a photo of the hand sticking out of the grave. As much as I hate to, I'll let her get as far as the tape."

"She'll want a quote from you."

"It won't mean anything. We don't have a positive ID yet."

"She'll also want an exclusive interview when this is over."

Stony stiffened enough to match his name. "I need your promise that she'll turn over all her research to my detectives."

"You have it."

A final growl sealed the deal. "I'll call the deputy at the front gate and tell her to let Lou Cooper pass. It's up to you to keep a leash on her."

Fen stepped to the back of Stony's vehicle and told his phone to call Lou.

"I'm crossing the river. Where do I go?"

"Slow down or you'll fly past the driveway. There's a deputy at the front gate. The sheriff's calling her with instructions to let you in. I had to do some fancy talking to get you on the property. You'll be the only reporter allowed on the ranch. I also got the sheriff to agree to give you an interview."

The hesitation was three seconds too long. "What kind of deal did you have to make?"

"I'll tell you when you get here. It's not that bad."

"That tells me it's not good either."

"I need to go. I haven't spoken to Bailey yet."

"Why not?"

"I've been busy keeping you out of the river."

"Huh?"

"You ask too many questions."

"That's how I make my living."

Fen had said all he needed to, so he disconnected the call to avoid a verbal jousting match.

Instead of staying in the cab, Bailey and a young woman sat on the tailgate of Bailey's truck. They were inside the crime scene tape, but none of the officers made a move to stop him from entering.

Bailey pushed off with her hands and greeted him. "How long do you think we'll have to stay here?"

He ignored the question for the time being. "Aren't you going to introduce me?"

"Oops. Sorry."

The young woman launched herself off the tailgate and thrust out a hand. "I'm Ren Duvant, and you're Fen Maguire. It's so cool to meet you. You're all Bailey's been talking about. I think you're the best landscape painter in the state. I paint murals, mostly on buildings. It doesn't pay that much, but who cares as long as you're doing what you love? Don't you agree?"

It had been a while since Fen met anyone who could cram so many sentences into one breath. Before she could start her next sentence, he said, "My painting has taken me to some great small towns, like Georgetown."

She held up a hand. "Wait, Georgetown isn't that small anymore. Have you seen all the building going on?"

Before he could get an answer in, she continued. "Anyway, about my murals. The city looks for ways to tell stories about the town's history on the sides of old buildings and give us young artists a chance. I think it's because they have money to spend because so many people are moving here. It's a win-win arrangement."

Fen took stock of Ren Duvant, great-granddaughter of the man believed to be in the ground not far away. She wore baggy gray sweatpants and a black hooded sweatshirt. A beautiful mane of wavy auburn hair hung down past her shoulders to mid-back. The high-top tennis shoes spoke to her youthfulness. On second look, they had wedge heels. Each piece of clothing bore splotches of paint, advertising her trade. She was the picture of an independent spirit.

He tuned in to Ren's chatter again.

"It's such a bummer about Great-Grandpa. I was almost over the sadness. Now I have to start all over." She paused. "Maybe not. I had to force myself to cry at the funeral. My mom says I was born with my giggle box turned on. Bailey says you'll find out who killed him. That's rad. I bet my grandpa will offer a reward."

Fen needed to lower her expectations. "The sheriff is in charge, not me."

Ren showed she wasn't an airhead when she said, "The sheriff messed up by saying Great-Grandpa died in the fire. I knew he wasn't in the house, but no one listened to me."

"Who did you tell?"

"Mostly the family, but also the cops." She used her fingers to check off names. "I told Grandpa Gil, Uncle Chance, Uncle Les, and Dad. Mom believed me, but most people around here don't listen to her either. Grandma Prissy believed me, but she used tarot cards. Does that count?"

Ren rattled on. "I don't know if I'm supposed to call her Prissy or Grandma. She goes by Duvant, but Grandpa says they never married. She was his third wife if they really were married."

"Did you tell your dad you thought your great-grandfather didn't die in the fire?"

"Oh, yeah. Him, too. His name is Robert Duvant, if you didn't already know. He's cool. Cut me loose to paint after high school and never hassled me to go to college."

Fen realized that Ren was a great source of Duvant family information. He fixed his gaze on the silver stud in Ren's nose.

"Do you know why the sheriff believed your great-grandfather died in the fire?"

"Yeah. They found human ashes. Those were Great-Grandma Duvant's. Great-Grandpa was tight with money and had her cremated. She was in a wooden box instead of a fire-proof urn." She looked at the sky. "I don't think it would have mattered. There was nothing much left of their home."

A wide smile crossed Ren's face. "Great-Grandpa was an absolute hoot. He called the box he put Great-Grandma in his 'hot-momma box.' She lived up to the name, even after she died."

Ren reinforced the description by shaking her shoulders in a shimmy. "That must be where I get my rhythm. I bet she could…"

Bailey interrupted. "Tell Fen about what you told the cops."

Ren ended her impromptu dance. "I told Bart Hill. He told a detective." She rolled her eyes. "That old goat treated me like I was a four-year-old making up a fairy tale."

That didn't come as a surprise to Fen. The existence of human ashes made the verdict of accidental death an easy call. Perhaps too easy. Case closed. Put the file away and move on to the next one.

More vehicles arrived, a signal to Fen that he needed to hurry. "Investigators will be here soon. They'll separate you two. Don't be surprised if they take you to the sheriff's department and ask you a bunch of questions. Be polite." He looked at Ren. "Be yourself, and it won't take long before they'll send you home."

Ren said, "They messed up, didn't they?"

Fen didn't answer. "If they pressure you too hard or accuse you of a crime, tell them you demand to talk to a lawyer. Hopefully, they'll limit their questions to your activities today. When in doubt, say, 'I don't know,' or 'I don't remember.'"

Fen's prophecy concerning detectives separating Bailey and Ren came to pass in a matter of minutes. He barely had time to tell Bailey to invite her new friend to their rental for supper.

Lou's Camry joined a sea of first responders. He met her on the unrestricted side of the tape. She wasted no time in quizzing him. "Where's the body and where's the sheriff?"

He pointed. "The body's near the creek bed. You can't see it from here." His finger shifted to a clump of men in uniforms. "Sheriff Rhoads is the man with four stars on his lapels. I'll try to get him over here, but it may be a long wait."

Her scowl expressed displeasure. "There's only two things wrong." She held up a finger. "There's nothing for me to photograph except cop cars." A thumb joined the index finger. "Two. He's going to put me off until he's ready to leave for the night. Did you notice how he turned his back on me when we started talking?"

She scanned the area within the perimeter of the yellow tape. "Absolutely nothing of genuine interest. You'd better have something more than Bailey's truck and a ditch that I can't see into."

"I do," said Fen. "But you can't print it yet."

She tented her hands on her hips. "What did you promise?"

"That you'd make the sheriff and his investigators look good, even though they screwed up. You can put whatever you want in your book after the sheriff's out of office."

Lou's eyes rolled. Fen said, "Count to ten before you tear into me."

"One, two, ten. You jerk. I'll not be a party to a cover-up."

"I'm not asking you to. Here are the facts: Two young

artists found what's believed to be the skeletal remains of an unknown person on the Duvant ranch. The Williamson County sheriff's office is investigating."

Lou took a step toward him. "What's the complete story?"

Fen pointed toward Ren. "That's Ren Duvant, great-granddaughter to Gilbert Duvant who the police believe died in a house fire over six months ago. The police investigators closed the case because fire investigators ruled it an accident after they found human ashes in the home. Ren tried to tell the cops the ashes belonged to her great-grandmother. They didn't listen to her."

"Why not?"

"You'll find out tonight when Bailey brings her new friend to the home I rented." Fen grinned. "You'll like her. Her tongue wags like a dog's tail."

It came as a surprise when Sheriff Rhoads walked to the crime tape and motioned for Fen to join him.

"Are you ready to meet Lou Cooper?"

"Let's get this over with."

Chapter Ten

Fen punched in a code that unlocked the door to the three-bedroom frame home on a street two blocks from the courthouse square. A whirling sound signaled the bolt moved and he stepped across the threshold. He nodded his approval as he entered the remodeled, updated 1950's home.

Because he was the first to arrive, Fen had his choice of bedrooms. The females would share a bathroom in the hall, while he took the largest bedroom with an en suite bathroom. This would avoid any awkward meetings in the hours between midnight and dawn. Being the eldest of the group removed any guilt about taking the only bedroom with an attached bathroom. The king-size bed was an added perk of rapidly approaching mid-fifties.

It surprised him when Lou arrived a short time later. Smoke wasn't coming out of her ears, but it should have been. She came in with a travel bag in one hand and a valise carrying her laptop in the other. Windows rattled when she kicked the door shut. "Where's my bedroom?"

"There's two open. Take your pick. Mine's at the end of the hall."

He watched from the recliner as she turned into the first room, backed out, and went into the room he'd selected at the end of the hall and backed out of that one. Into the remaining door, she stomped.

Lou soon returned. "You took the one with the bathroom. That figures."

"You can have it."

"Forget it. You're footing the bill." She cast her gaze down the hall. "You're probably like my last husband. He'd drink two glasses of water before we went to bed. I didn't get an uninterrupted night's sleep for three years."

Fen put a more chipper tone to his next question. "How was the interview with the sheriff?"

Lou almost threw herself onto the sofa. "Other than being a man who hates anyone with press credentials, he's a lovely charmer, an absolute prince."

Fen groaned. "Didn't he talk to you?"

She threw a look his way that could scorch concrete. "Sounds came from his mouth, but they carried not a smidgen of information. Talk about a word salad. The only thing missing was dressing and croutons."

Lou continued before he could make a comment. "Guess what he did after he told me absolutely nothing?"

"Do I have to?"

"His parting shot was to move the crime scene perimeter back. He was such a coward he made a deputy tell me to move my car."

"How far did you have to move?"

"A quarter mile, and I'm not exaggerating."

Fen gave his head a tiny nod. "Did he leave the original tape in place?"

"Yes."

"Stony established a secondary perimeter. It's not unheard of."

"He did it on purpose."

Fen had heard enough. "You don't know that. I did the same thing a couple of times and it had nothing to do with obstructing the press. My situation called for it, and he must have determined his did, too."

Lou pointed at him. "You're defending him."

Fen matched her accusatory gaze with one of his own. "Lou, I don't know what your problem is, but you need to get over it. In case you don't remember, Chuck and Candy are paying you to do research. That you get to sell stories to news outlets and collect inside information for future books is an added benefit. If I tell you to go easy on the cops, there's a good reason for it."

Lou rose from the couch, stormed to her room, and slammed the door. He wondered if he'd come down too hard on her. On the one hand, Lou was what the old-timers called a tough cookie. On the other, she'd never reacted so violently to obstacles. In fact, she thrived on overcoming them.

He puffed out his cheeks and blew. His thoughts shifted. Ren had given him more Duvant family information than he expected, but it was still incomplete. He needed Lou for this case. She had a reporter's desire to uncover family secrets. He'd also promised the sheriff the research Lou had already done. If she bolted, he'd be in a pickle.

The memory of him as a seven-year-old who prided himself on his skill with watercolors and cartoon characters sprang to mind. One day his father gave him a roller, a three-inch-wide paintbrush and a bucket of battleship-gray paint. With all the concentration of a surgeon, he dutifully applied the paint to the decking of their cabin's front porch.

Pride welled up in him as he neared the end of the job until he realized the only section left to paint was a cluster of boards against the wall of the cabin. He looked down in horror at his tennis shoes on a tiny island of faded white boards in a sea of gray.

His father thought it hilarious. Footprints and a rectangle of unpainted wood remained until the cabin was sold after his parents died. A testament to what happens when pride clouds a mind.

Fen ran a hand down his face. He hoped this wouldn't be another time he'd find himself painted into a corner.

The knock on the door took Fen's gaze to the front door. He hollered, "It's unlocked. Come on in, Bailey."

Another knock and Fen brought the recliner's footrest down. "I said it's unlocked. Turn the handle and push."

The knob on the inside turned, and the door opened, but only an inch. A woman's voice sounded, "Yoo-hoo... Mr. Maguire? It's Sunny Day. We met at the Monument Cafe this morning."

Fen's day wasn't improving. He couldn't even respond to a knock on the door without embarrassing himself. He sprung to his feet. "Sorry, Ms. Day. I thought you were someone else. Please come in."

She flipped the apology away with two words. "No problem. I hope I'm not intruding."

"Not at all. I'd offer you a drink, but I haven't seen the kitchen yet. I suppose there's water."

"There's tea and coffee. Which would you prefer?" She then chuckled. "I should explain. I run a property management company and this house is one of our properties." She corrected herself. "I'm not the owner, just the manager. I meant to come by earlier and make sure the cleaners did a satisfactory job."

"It looks great to me."

Sunny spoke as she walked. "Let me show you the kitchen and make you something to drink. There's something I'd like to discuss with you."

He followed her like an obedient dog. They passed a large dining table and turned into a galley-style kitchen with new appliances. "Have you seen the backyard and patio yet?" asked Sunny.

"I picked out a bed and didn't make it past the recliner on my way back through." He walked to the French doors. "It's very nice. Did you oversee the renovations?"

The sound of running water caused him to shift his gaze to the kitchen. Sunny looked his way as she filled the reservoir of a single-serve brewer. "You have your choice of this single-serve brewer or a regular coffee pot so you can make coffee or tea whenever you're ready. I've supplied regular coffee, decaf, or tea. Ice dispenses from the door of the fridge."

"Thanks. That takes care of two of life's necessities: coffee and iced tea."

"Amen to that. I'm having a cup of coffee. What will you have?"

"The same. Black. Of course, that may be my only choice since I haven't been to the store yet."

"You'll find basic condiments and staples in the cabinet. You can at least sweeten your tea."

"That's a nice perk. I've found Airbnb kitchens are not created equal."

She set a steaming cup of coffee on the table and smiled. "I wouldn't expect you to drink it any way but black."

"Why?"

"Ten years as a highway patrolman and another ten as sheriff of Newman County. I bet you like donuts, too."

Fen wiggled his eyebrows. "Someone's been checking up on me."

She tented her hands on shapely hips. "You guys have it so lucky. You can eat whatever you like. Donuts go straight to my caboose."

"What about the MONUMENT's chocolate pie? That's been one of my favorites for years. Anytime I had to come for a training at the Highway Patrol academy, I made time for a piece of pie."

"That's strictly off limits. I can't even look at it."

Fen and Sunny seated themselves at the kitchen table with mugs of steaming coffee in front of them. Sunny spoke in a tone of pretend offense. "I hate to do it, but Sheriff Rhoads is in for a scolding."

"Why's that?"

"The sheriff didn't tell me about your careers in law enforcement. I stumbled on it when I was researching your art. Is that what really brings you to town?"

It would have been easy to tell Sunny he was working with Sheriff Rhoads, but something kept him from it. Instead, he gave the simple answer. "I came to paint the San Gabriel. It will be an addition to my Texas Rivers collection."

Sunny tapped the handle of her mug with a manicured nail. "That's the reason I'm here. When Bart heard we had a famous artist in town, he insisted I contact you. He's very familiar with your work and wants to explore the possibility of a showing in his gallery."

The request intrigued him, but he needed more information. "It's an interesting offer." His mind shifted to Bailey and Ren. "I have a protégé who'll be staying here while I paint the river. She'll be looking for scenes to paint too. It would be good for her to experience a gallery show."

Sunny covered his hand with hers. "You've made my day... no, my entire week. Bart will be so pleased. He's intent on changing this county."

The tilt of Fen's head asked a question without having to use words.

"Don't misunderstand me. He loves the county's history. Do you know the Chisholm Trail went through Georgetown? In fact, the cattle were driven past where the courthouse now stands, just a few blocks from here. I bet they grazed in what's now the yard."

Fen took up the story. "Mr. Hill must understand how a unique history helps sell an area. Blend the old with the new and sell both."

"You took the words right out of my mouth."

"I'd like to meet Mr. Hill," said Fen.

Sunny spoke with absolute certainty. "Oh, you will. I guarantee it."

She rose and took her mug to the sink, washed and dried it. "I hate to run, but there are a dozen more things I have to do tonight."

Fen and Sunny were crossing the living room when the front door flew open. Bailey and Ren exploded into the home, talking over each other.

Ren was the first to speak. "Hey, Sunny. I didn't expect to see you here. This is Bailey Madison. She's an artist who has her own studio. It's in an apartment over Mr. Maguire's garage." A look of revelation opened her eyes wider. "Hey, that's a studio in a studio. How gnarly is that?"

Ren barely took a breath. "Bailey and I had to go to the sheriff's department. We gave formal statements about what we found. It wasn't as rad as I thought it would be."

"Why were you there?" asked Sunny.

"You haven't heard?"

"Heard what?"

"We found a body at Grandpa's ranch." She held up both

hands like she was commanding a train to stop. "Check that last statement. We don't know if it was a whole body. The only thing sticking out of the ground was part of an arm and a hand. I think it's Great-Grandpa, but the police told me not to say that."

Fen was standing behind Sunny and couldn't see her reaction, but he heard her gasp. A shaky voice said. "Where was this?"

"Beside a teeny-tiny creek by the river."

Sunny stood ramrod straight. "Was your grandfather there?"

"Not when we left. The detective told me not to worry about him or anyone else. He sort of got mad at me. Probably because my tongue flaps like a flag in a windstorm. That's what my mom says."

Bailey gave Ren a gentle nudge. "If we're going to talk, let's get out of the doorway."

Ren looked at Sunny. "We're going to 600 Degrees Pizza. Do you want to come with us?"

"No, thanks. I need to call your grandfather and make sure he's all right."

Fen waited until Sunny was out the door before he turned to question the two artists. "How was the interview?"

"Short for me," said Bailey. "I did what you told me to do. They didn't like it that I kept saying 'I don't know,' but that's their problem. I told them why I was there, what I saw, and that I live and work with you."

Ren had walked to a painting that hung on the wall and examined it like a child looking at a bug. "If you're wondering why Sunny was interested in my grandpa, it's because they're dating. Do you think that's sweet or gross? I'm leaning toward gross. She's after his land."

Bailey asked, "Where's Lou? Her car's here."

"In her room," said Fen. "Get an extra pizza to go."

"Is she all right?"

Fen crossed fingers behind his back. "She's fine. You know how she is when there's research to do."

Chapter Eleven

The day's activities caught up with Fen. He walked to the recliner as if some unseen force had him by the hand and stared into space as images and words from the day ran laps in his mind. It had been a long and event-filled day and it wasn't over yet.

"Hey!" said Bailey. She stood in front of him, looking down. "What's wrong with you?"

He shifted his gaze up to her face. "I'm experiencing sensory overload."

"You picked a bad time for that. We're starving."

"Call and get it to go."

Ren chimed in. "Great idea. I have 600 Degrees on speed dial. It's close enough that we can walk."

Fen reached for his wallet, but Bailey stopped him. "I'll put it on my card. We'll settle later. I have a feeling there will be many more charges before we go home."

Ren was already at the door with her hand on the doorknob. "Let's scoot, Bailey. Mr. Fen looks like my dad does after a late night of playing on Sixth Street in Austin."

Bailey spoke over her shoulder. "I'll get salads for you and Lou. I know how you old folks need your roughage."

The words barely registered with Fen. He pulled the handle on the recliner, raised his feet, and closed his eyes. The revelation that Sunny Day was dating Gil Duvant, a man about thirty years her senior, had blindsided him. Ren's theory that she was after the land fit nicely into having a motive for killing Gilbert Senior. Kill the patriarch and make it look like an accident. Next, marry Gil and gain access to the land. Sunny could then either wait for Gil to die or hasten his demise.

Fen opened his eyes as the sound of footsteps brought him out of his trip to Never-Never land, the place of half-awake, half-asleep imagination.

"Were you asleep?" asked Lou.

"Not exactly. Ren said something that sent my mind flying off a cliff. She said a woman named Sunny Day is dating Gil Duvant. I moved Sunny into the place of suspect number one on my list. With my eyes open, things look different."

Lou took a seat on the couch. "Who was the woman I heard you talking to?"

"That was Sunny. She runs the property management company that rents out this house."

"I'll get to work on finding out what I can about her."

"Thanks."

An awkward silence settled over the room. Fen and Lou spoke over each other at the same time. Fen held up a hand. "Ladies first."

Lou preceded her words with a deep breath. "I want to apologize for being such a witch. There's no good excuse, but let me tell you what's going on. I found out this week that my sister's daughter has a serious heart murmur that requires surgery."

Fen involuntarily sucked in enough air for two normal

breaths. An image of his wife in a hospital bed flashed in front of him in sepia-muted colors. The heart monitor beeped infrequently, then stopped. Her body had rejected the transplant after a few years and she'd refused consideration for another. Sally believed she'd already had her extra time. She wanted someone else to have the chance to live a normal life.

Fen tried to swallow.

Lou looked at Fen, her face pale and stricken. "Oh, I'm sorry. I didn't mean to bring up bad memories. I wasn't thinking."

He corralled his emotions. That was the past and this was the here and now. Lou needed to talk and he needed to listen. "It's all right." He took a breath. "What kind of surgery are they talking about?"

"A valve replacement."

"Remind me, how old is your niece?"

"Sixteen."

"Doesn't she live out of state?"

"She did. They moved back to Dallas."

Fen didn't sugarcoat his words. "It's a serious surgery, but the success rate is very high. At most, there's a two percent mortality rate. For a young woman, it's only one percent."

Lou snapped back. "I'm well aware of the risks and percentages. Research is what I do for a living." She closed her eyes and allowed several seconds to right her emotional ship. "Sorry. I can't bear the thought of them stopping her heart and having to shock her back to life."

Instead of moving on or offering some platitude, Fen held his words inside.

Lou continued to speak in quick sentences. "I know I sound like a fool, but I can't help it. She's my only niece, and she's so young."

"Do you want to sit out this investigation?"

Lou leaned forward. "What I'd like for you to do is keep me busy. I'll need off for the surgery, but that's not for two more weeks."

Fen rubbed his hands together like a mad scientist. "If you want to stay busy, you've come to the right place. The first thing I need for you to do is send all the background information you've collected to Sheriff Rhoads."

Lou reeled back and crossed her arms. "That jerk kept me from getting anything newsworthy today. Give me one good reason for me turning over my research."

Fen faced the challenge head-on. "You know how we work, so don't pretend that you don't. I had to make a deal with the sheriff to get you close to the crime scene. You were the only reporter allowed on the property. I agree it was a lousy deal, but it's a baby step to building trust between us and the sheriff. We're going to need that trust to get access to information as the investigation progresses."

A low grumble sounded from Lou, but she didn't follow up with words.

Fen kept talking at a steady pace. "I want us both to coach Bailey on how to get information out of Ren and a deputy named Cory Blane. Ren likes to talk and Cory doesn't. Both can be sources of information if we play our cards right."

Lou tilted her head. "Are we working under the assumption that the body Bailey and Ren found is Gilbert Duvant?"

"That's correct. We don't have to wait for a formal identification if we can get Ren to find out from Cory Blane if Billy was in the same grave."

"Who's Billy?"

"Gilbert's dog."

Lou sat up straight. "You know how the murder took place."

"I have a theory," said Fen.

"I want to hear it."

"Someone either lured or abducted Gilbert Duvant out of his home. They went to the spot you were at today. That's where they killed Gilbert and his dog. They buried both near the creek that ran into the river. After that, there was plenty of time to fill Gilbert's home with propane and set some sort of time-delay igniter. That would allow them time to get well away from the explosion and subsequent fire. The investigators assumed Gilbert and Billy had perished in the fire and it reduced them to ashes."

"That's quite the theory," said Lou. "What if the dog isn't in the grave?"

Fen laced his fingers together. "It could still be Gilbert, but I'm counting on both being there."

He paused. "In the meantime, I want you to add to what we know about Gilbert Duvant, Gil, and his three ex-wives. Also, Gil's three sons, Chance, Les, and Robert. Robert is Ren's father."

Lou's face twisted as she asked, "Is Sunny Day that woman's real name?"

Fen shrugged. "That's for you to find out."

"One more question," said Lou.

Fen interrupted her before she could ask. "Do you know how many times you say that? It never turns out to be one more."

Lou chuckled. "Guilty as charged, Sheriff Maguire." She collected her thoughts. "Am I expected to share everything I discover in my research with the sheriff?"

"That wasn't our deal," said Fen. A conspirator's tone filled his words. "I'll need to give him enough to keep him satisfied, but his investigators need to earn their paychecks."

"That's better. I thought for a moment this was going to be a one-way street."

Fen picked up his phone and punched in Bailey's number. The roar of a crowded room sounded behind her voice. "We're still waiting for our order. It shouldn't be much longer. We're only three or four blocks away from you."

"Good. We're hungry." He took a breath. "This is your first assignment, and it's important. Get Ren to call Cory and find out if there was a dog buried with the body you found. We don't need to know details. Only if there was a human and a dog."

"Wait a minute. Let me step outside."

Fen waited until she spoke again.

"Okay, I'm fairly alone. If they found a dog, that would mean it's her great-grandpa."

"You're a smart young woman."

"If I were smart, I'd have thought of it first." She paused. "We're getting along pretty well. Do you think asking her to do that will make Ren back away?"

"Not if you do it right."

"How do I do it right?"

"You'll know if you did it wrong. She won't talk to you anymore."

A huff of exasperation came over the phone's speaker, followed by the call cutting off.

Lou looked at him. "You enjoy winding her up, don't you?"

"It's a game we play. Keeps us both on our toes. Don't worry; she'll have her revenge before we solve this murder."

Lou went to the kitchen in search of paper plates and napkins. She located both after going through what sounded like every drawer and cabinet. Fen stayed in the recliner until the sound of singing preceded the front door swinging open.

Ren's version of an upbeat tune ended as she announced, "Pizza! Get it while it's hot."

Fen threw a thumb over his shoulder. "Kitchen table. Lou has drinks poured. I hope you like water."

"Water works for me," said Ren.

Bailey wasn't as gracious. "I knew I should have picked up a soda. Oh well, if it's good enough for fish, it'll do for me."

Ren let out a raucous laugh. "I'll have to remember that line."

Bailey remembered her manners. "Lou, this is Ren Duvant. Ren, say hi to Lou. She's the best newspaper reporter in the state. You should see her fingers fly across the keyboard. She also writes books."

"How cool," said Ren. "A fellow creative. Artists and writers have so much in common. I'd be a writer if it weren't for all the words I'd have to use." She pretended to grasp a brush out of the air and make sweeping strokes with it. "My brush becomes an extension of my arm that's attached to my soul. It's like I lose control of it when I'm really in the flow."

Fen gave his head a nod. "You're speaking my language."

Ren's head jerked down and back up. "Isn't it the best feeling?" She spun in a circle. "I sometimes put in earbuds and paint all night." She paused and focused. "That doesn't work when I paint murals. There's never enough light no matter how many shop lights we set up. I tried it a few times, and it ended in a hot mess."

Fen was going to suggest they eat while the pizza was still hot, but Ren kept talking. "At least Billy wasn't with Great-Grandpa. It still makes me super sad."

Fen and Lou traded looks. Bailey turned so Ren couldn't see her wriggling eyebrows. She'd completed her assignment without alienating Ren and was duly proud of herself.

Fen cast his gaze to Ren. "Do you understand this means someone still could have killed your great-grandpa?"

"I already knew that. What I want to know is how you're going to solve it."

"All you have to do is answer our questions. Unlike the cops, we'll believe what you say."

"It's about time. Do you know how frustrating it is to be ignored?"

Bailey cut into the conversation. "You don't have to worry about that with any of us."

"That's good, because I'm not saying another word to any cop except Cory. They don't like to listen to him either."

Ren became even more animated. "They didn't believe me when I told them they'd found Great-Grandma's ashes and not Great-Grandpa's." Ren sealed her commitment with her right hand over her heart. "I couldn't feel Great-Grandpa's aura in his house. That's how I knew for sure."

Fen opened a pizza box. "First things first. Let's eat." He pushed the box toward Ren. She took two slices and passed it on. Before digging in she asked, "How can I help you find Great-Grandpa's killer?"

The question had already occurred to Fen, and what he hoped was a seed of inspiration was poking up. It was either that or a weed of confusion.

He looked at each expectant face at the table but settled his gaze on Ren. "I can't lie to the sheriff, but I don't have to answer unasked questions. For the time being, Lou and I will filter questions through Bailey. That way we can honestly say that you didn't tell us anything related to the case. Is that acceptable to you?"

"Fine with me," chirped Ren. "Do you want to know about my uncles or Prissy first? Prissy's a lot more interesting than Grandpa or my uncles."

Ren had a way of saying things that caught him off guard.

He needed to buy time. "It's been a long day for us old people," said Fen. "You decide and tell Bailey about them."

"That's awesomely awesome," said Ren as she spoke around a bite of pizza. "Bailey and I can have a slumber party."

Lou took over. "Do you need to get your car or have Bailey take you home before you two have a talk?"

"What car? What home? I have an e-bike and a backpack. I can zip around town at almost thirty miles an hour."

Fen asked, "Where do you sleep?"

"I mostly couch hop with friends and fellow artists. Uncle Les lets me stay with them, and so does Grandpa, but they try to preach to me about settling down."

Lou asked, "What's your idea of a slumber party?"

"What kind of bed is in Bailey's room?"

"Two twins," said Fen.

"That works, or I can sleep on the couch. The slumber party can be in either room."

Bailey spoke up. "That was easy."

Ren was finishing her second piece of pizza. "I'll walk over to Uncle Les's house and get my bike and backpack. It's not far and I think he's getting tired of me putting a dent in his couch."

Fen could see why. The idea of non-stop chatter didn't appeal to him, but he needed what Ren could deliver: inside information on the Duvant family. This would give him a leg up on the sheriff's detectives, which would please Lou and Bailey. He had to admit, the thought of solving the crime put a spring in his step, too.

Chapter Twelve

F en intended to start his truck to warm up the engine while he ducked back inside and finished his cup of coffee. He made it inside his truck when the ringing of his cell phone interrupted his plan. His index finger swiped the screen. "Good morning, Chuck. Isn't this early for a lawyer to be calling?"

"Candy and I had to get a jump on the day." He paused. "What's that noise? It sounds like a hay baler."

"A cold diesel engine. I had my time with Sally, drank a cup and a half of coffee, and thought I'd go somewhere to get breakfast."

"Try Just Love. It's a coffee shop in the Wolf Ranch shopping center. If you want excellent coffee, friendly service, and something a little different, try it. I recommend their Flying Pig. It's a waffle stuffed with bacon, sausage, and egg. It comes with either maple syrup or sausage gravy."

"Sounds good. Now tell me the real reason you called."

"I wanted you to know Sheriff Rhoads has his hackles up. He didn't like Lou's attitude when she interviewed him yesterday. He had to move the perimeter back to keep her from getting too close to the grave."

"Stony wasn't too keen on having a reporter there, not even one affiliated with me. But I think he may have exaggerated the situation. As for Lou's attitude, she was definitely in a rare mood. She's worried sick about her niece needing a replacement valve in her heart."

Candy broke in. "We hadn't heard about that. It sounds serious."

"It is to Lou. I didn't stick around for her interview with the sheriff, but I can imagine how it went. The timing couldn't have been worse."

"Why's that?" asked Candy.

"The sheriff's detectives didn't do Stony any favors by calling a murder an accident six months ago."

Chuck asked, "Are you sure the person in the grave is Gilbert Duvant?"

"It's not official and won't be for as long as the sheriff can stretch it out. Up to now, everyone thought Gilbert's dog had died in the fire. I'm not so sure, and he wasn't in the grave. The sheriff wants to keep any mention of Gilbert out of the press to give his team a jump on correcting their mistakes."

"I guess Lou's not happy about that, either."

Fen took in a breath of cool morning air. "It gets worse. Gilbert's great-granddaughter tried to tell investigators the ashes they thought belonged to Gilbert were his wife's. Of course, they didn't listen to her. If it's Gilbert in the grave, she will have been proven right and they will have egg on their face."

"No wonder Stony's upset. Calling a murder an accident could cost him votes in the next election. Be careful how you handle this and keep Lou reigned in."

"I'm meeting with Stony this morning to give him Lou's

research notes. That might save his detectives some time and get us back in his good graces."

"Tread lightly with Stony," said Chuck. "He's one of the good guys."

Phone calls to or from Chuck and Candy rarely lasted more than a few minutes. After the call ended, a thought ran a lap around Fen's mind. What if he and his crew could solve the murder before identification of the body came back from the coroner? Nah. That would take a miracle.

His mind kept whirling. They might not solve it that quickly, but he'd give even odds of them succeeding before the sheriff's detectives.

Fen left the truck running and jogged back into the house. He pushed the front door open with enough force that it slammed against the stopper and bounced back at him. The footfalls of his boots sounded like drumbeats as he quick-walked across the hardwood floor to Bailey's room. This time, he held onto the knob as he entered without knocking.

Bailey bolted upright. "What's wrong?"

"Nothing. Go back to sleep."

He went to the twin bed on the other side of the room and saw a riot of auburn hair splayed across a pillow. "Ren... Ren, wake up."

"Huh?"

"Wake up. I have a question for you."

"Wha... What is it?"

He wasn't sure she was awake enough to understand but tried anyway. "Did your great-grandfather have any teeth when he died?"

"Huh?"

He tried again. "I need to know if your great-grandfather had any teeth."

"It's too early."

"I know it is, but this is important." He increased the volume. "Did your great-grandfather Duvant have any teeth?"

Ren cracked open an eye. "Dentures, but he only put them in to eat."

"Full dentures? No teeth at all?"

Ren pulled in her top and bottom lips to make it look like she was toothless. "Lost the last tooth before I was born."

"Thanks. Go back to sleep."

He didn't see the pillow coming that Bailey launched at him. It did no harm but sent his Stetson flying. "That's what you get for waking us up in the middle of the night. What's so important about false teeth?"

"I'll tell you later." He eased Bailey's door shut and scurried toward the kitchen to retrieve his coffee.

Lou sat at the table wearing a full-length robe, with steam rising from a mug. She didn't bother looking up when Fen said, "Good morning."

He retrieved his mug and popped it in the microwave for a warm-up. "It's a nice crisp morning. Not a cloud in sight."

She gave him a sideways glance. "Why are you in such a good mood?"

"I'm going to get the sheriff back on our side."

"Oh?" She looked into her cup. "How?"

"I asked Ren if her great-grandfather had any teeth."

Lou looked at him like he'd grown another head.

Fen pressed on. "With no teeth, the police can't check dental records to get a positive ID. That means we have somewhere between three days and a week to find the killer before DNA results come back. That's assuming the sheriff releases the identity of the body right away. My guess is he's not in a hurry, and we have a full week."

Lou folded her hands together in front of her mug. "What difference does it make?"

Fen retrieved his mug from the microwave and sat at the head of the table. "If I hadn't stopped you, how would you have written yesterday's story?"

"Heavy on facts."

"And what would those facts lead people to believe?"

Lou sat up straight. "That the sheriff's department did a lousy job investigating a murder."

"Exactly. Now, think carefully before you speak. Let's say the sheriff can put a lid on the story for the next week. In the meantime, either we or the sheriff names the person or persons who killed Gilbert Duvant. How would that story be different?"

Lou gave him a squint-eyed response. "You're a sneaky man, Fen Maguire. You're willing to sacrifice a perfectly good story of police incompetence to save the reputation of one of your good old boys."

"That's because Stony *is* one of the good guys."

Lou shook her head. "The best cops don't hide the truth."

Fen grinned. "All right, he's only ninety-nine percent good. We're not talking about lies or corruption here."

"I wouldn't rate him that high, but I get your point. What do you want me to do about it?"

"Nothing that you weren't already planning to do, except make sure Bailey presses Ren for information. We're up against a deadline and need to get moving. I'm going to talk to Stony this morning and see how hard he's pressing his detectives."

Fen stood. "I'm also going for breakfast. Do you want to go with me?"

Lou shook her head. "Ren told me about a place near the square called Galaxy Bakery. They're supposed to have the best scones in the world. I'll do something with myself, walk there, and get the girls something special. They should have come to life by the time I get back. I hope to have more information on family members by noon."

"Noon would be good. We could start interviews this afternoon."

"We?"

He finished his coffee and put the mug in the sink. "Mostly me, but with only a week I may need help."

"Who do you interview first?" asked Lou as she stood.

"I'll start at the top with the newest patriarch, Gil Duvant. See if Ren can arrange a meeting. If she can't or won't, I'll think of something else."

Lou asked, "Have you checked your email today?"

"Not yet."

"I finished updating the files on family members last night instead of joining the girl's slumber party. Give them to the sheriff or whomever you want."

"Thanks, Lou. I'm sorry this isn't working out where you can write ongoing stories."

"Get out of here before I change my mind." She wrapped her hand around her mug but didn't lift it. "Tell the sheriff my silence will cost him an exclusive when they arrest the killer."

The onboard computer showed the route Fen needed to take to get to the coffee shop. He'd driven a block and a half when his phone signaled an incoming call. The screen read it was from the sheriff's department.

Fen answered by stating his name.

"Sheriff Rhoads would like to move your appointment with him. Is there any way you can come to his office now?"

"I'm about six blocks away."

It took longer to walk from his truck to the building than it did to drive. He'd miscalculated the distance and was only four blocks away. An officer whisked him through security and into the private sanctum of the sheriff.

Stony was clean-shaven and wore a starched uniform, but the dark circles under his eyes told a tale of lack of sleep. He was on his feet when Fen crossed the room. "Morning, Fen."

Fen received the obligatory handshake. "I notice you didn't say it was a good morning."

"It might be if I hear that brassy reporter working with you hasn't filed a story about Gilbert Duvant's body being found in a grave when he should be a pile of ashes."

"Don't forget about Billy, his dog," said Fen. It was a verbal punch below the belt but with a purpose. He wanted Stony to know that Lou could write a story that would expose his detectives for their less-than-enthusiastic work.

Stony pulled a hand down his face. "Who'd she sell the story to?"

"No one. All Lou wants is an exclusive interview with you when you arrest Gilbert's killer."

Stony went back to the other side of his desk and motioned for Fen to sit. "I can hold out for—"

"About a week," said Fen.

Stony leaned back in his chair. "It seems we're walking in each other's shadow. The official version is two out-of-town visitors found human remains near the San Gabriel downstream from the Highway 29 bridge. An investigation as to identity is ongoing."

Fen nodded his approval. "Short, factual, and vague. I like it."

Stony glanced at the door behind Fen. "None of this would have happened if I hadn't been in such a hurry to close the case."

"Were you getting pressure from someone in particular?"

"Gilbert's son, Gil, was on me to close the case. He wanted

to have the funeral and get back to work. Just like his father, Gil doesn't believe in wasting daylight."

"First he pushed you to close the case, then after the will was read, he began pushing you to find his dad's killer." Fen shook his head. "Quite the turn around."

"Yeah, it would have saved us all some headaches if old man Gilbert hadn't put that six month wait clause in his will."

Fen brought the conversation back on point. "Well, we can't change that, so we'll do our best to find his killer quickly. Lou gave me her background files on the Duvant family members. Do you want me to forward those to you or someone else?"

"Me," said Stony without hesitation. "I want to review what's in them and compare them to what my detectives did in the original investigation. I may have to peel the bark off one or two of them."

Fen said, "You realize my team and yours might overlap. Is that going to be a problem?"

The sheriff took his time answering. "Are you wanting to interview all the family members?"

Fen gave his head a quick nod. "I thought I'd start with Gil Duvant."

"Give my detectives a one-day head start on all potential suspects. I'll tell them you and your team are following your own investigation at your own pace. After today, it's whoever gets to them first. If they complain, I'll remind them they've had over six months to realize their mistakes and correct them."

It wasn't the answer Fen wanted to hear, but at least the detectives would know the sheriff approved of Fen's parallel investigation.

On the way to his truck, Fen's phone rang again. Normally, he could count his daily phone calls on one hand and have fingers to spare. Lou's name appeared on the screen. "Lou," was all he could say before she cut him off.

"Thelma's here. She rousted the girls out of bed and has them unloading a week's worth of groceries. If she's staying, I'm leaving."

Chapter Thirteen

Lou was waiting in the driveway with hands on her hips when Fen arrived. He hadn't expected Thelma to show up uninvited. It was a major miscalculation on his part as she had a habit of making unannounced appearances. Her excuse was to ensure he and Bailey received Thelma's version of a nutritionally balanced diet. Lou was pretty much on her own, which she didn't mind. There wasn't animosity between the reporter and the housekeeper, but Lou didn't live under Fen's roof and didn't count as family.

Fen closed the door to his truck, walked straight to Lou, and said, "Here's what I want you to do. Take your list of all family members and go to the courthouse. Get dates of marriages and divorces of all Duvant family members. When I say all, I mean everyone, from Gilbert down to Ren or any cousins she may have. Be sure to ask Ren if there were any quickie marriages that were annulled in the Duvant woodpile."

Fen continued. "Next, I want to know all children in the Duvant bloodline. That includes everyone with even the slightest chance now, or in the future, of receiving an inheritance from Gil Duvant or his survivors."

Lou's hands had dropped to her sides. Curiosity seemed to replace anger. "You're working the money angle for Gilbert's murder. Do you have any proof yet?"

Fen ignored the question. "Put extra effort into finding all you can about Priscilla Duvant."

"Prissy is what Ren called her," said Lou. "From what Bailey's new best friend says, she's unique. If that's Ren's assessment, she must be something else."

"Two more," said Fen. "Sunny Day and Bart Hill. It may be my imagination, but they looked chummy in the restaurant the day before yesterday. That's strange for a woman who is supposed to be dating Gil with wedding bells in her future."

Lou cocked her head. "Is this busy work to keep me from ranting about Thelma?"

Fen glanced at the front porch before bringing his gaze back to Lou. "Thelma will be gone when you finish your research today."

"I can't stay here while she's cooking. The first thing she did was open the windows and turn on the air conditioner. It's like a meat locker inside."

"There are coffee shops nearby and a public library. Take your pick. I'll make sure Thelma is on the road home before dark. It's best if we all leave her alone today and let her feel like we need her."

Lou issued her first smile of the day. "I see what you're up to, and I think it's a brilliant idea. Having Thelma's precooked meals ready to heat and serve isn't such a bad thing. It sure beats cold sandwiches and cereal, which is what I usually eat."

Lou walked ahead of him into the house. She went directly to her bedroom while Fen went into the dining room. Bailey and Ren were both wrapped in fleece throws, clutching mugs of coffee with both hands. He glanced into the kitchen where Thelma was on her knees, looking into the depths of a lower cabinet.

Fen looked at the two shivering girls and jerked his head to the left, a sign for them to follow him. Chairs scraped against the floor and the three were soon in Bailey's bedroom. As with Lou, he wasted no time in putting things to rights.

"Ren," he began. "I'd like for you to get me an appointment with Prissy, preferably this morning. Can you do that?"

"Don't see why not. She's a night owl like me and won't be up for at least another hour."

"What else do you want us to do?"

"Go someplace and get a nice, hot breakfast."

Bailey shook her head. "We tried that. Thelma said we needed to stay here until she put her food in us and got our day off to a proper start."

"I'll take care of Thelma. You two get out of here and spend the day talking and painting. I'll catch up with you this afternoon."

His gaze shifted back and forth between Ren and Bailey as he spoke. "We need to get serious about finding the person responsible for killing Ren's great-grandfather. I met with the sheriff this morning. He wants us to give him a one-day head start on interviewing family members. I wanted to talk to Ren's grandfather first, but that will have to wait until tomorrow."

"I haven't called him yet," said Ren.

"Good. See if you can set me up for tomorrow morning. The earlier, the better."

"He alternates between restaurants. I'll find out which one he'll go to."

"Perfect. Thanks for helping us."

Ren's eyes flashed with anticipation. "This is so cool, but kind of yucky at the same time." She wrinkled a brow. "I'm sort of between jobs right now and don't have a mural to paint. I don't mind watching Bailey paint, but I'll need to go to the craft store and pick up a canvas if I'm to produce anything."

Bailey spoke before Fen could. "I have everything you need in my truck."

"That's totally rad. What do you want me to paint?"

Fen thought about it. "What's your favorite memory of your great-grandfather?"

Ren didn't have to think. "Great-Grandma's peach pie and the way my great-grandpa danced with her whenever she baked one. I never asked what made peach pie so special to them, but he sure came alive during peach season."

Fen swallowed hard. "Go to the ranch, stand where their house used to be, and paint that memory."

"But I'll cry."

Fen gave his head a slow nod. "So will others when they see it. Art is supposed to awaken the soul."

Fen walked through the living room, past the dining room, and into the kitchen. Thelma met him with, "It's a good thing I brought my large cast iron skillet. All this place has are those no-stick pans. They don't last six months."

Fen stood ramrod straight and gave her a look he'd perfected as a state trooper. He called it his *you're guilty and you know it* look.

Thelma was familiar with the look and what it meant, but she wasn't going down without a fight. "Don't be givin' me that. I'm saving you money and keeping all three of you healthy. There's no telling what kind of junk you'd eat if it weren't for me." She opened the refrigerator door and pointed. "See that? Left-over pizza and not a sprig of salad in sight. If you keep eating like that, your gut will shut down within three days. You know what a grump you are when your plumbin' backs up."

He didn't answer.

Thelma tried a different angle. "Bailey told me the name of this rental and how to find it on my computer. I hadn't planned on her having company. Surely that Ren gal has a home to go to."

Fen shook his head. "Ren's helping us on the case. Someone killed her great-grandfather and I need her here to find out about her family and others."

"There's the couch," said Thelma. "I could sleep there."

Fen's head went to the right and then the left, but only one time. Instead of continuing with his hard stare, he lifted his chin. "Do you know what would help us more than anything?"

"What's that?"

"Good, nutritious meals that we could heat and serve."

Thelma gave a grumpy utterance and spoke in a loud whisper. "That was my backup plan if you wouldn't let me stay. It's going to take me all day to cook everything."

"No problem," said Fen. "Lou left for the day and I've given the girls their assignments."

"That means you'll be leaving any minute, too."

Fen walked to her and placed a hand on her shoulder. "Not until you cook a breakfast that will last me until this afternoon."

"Biscuits are already in the oven. I thought I was cooking for two young ladies, but I heard the front door close, which means they have other plans. You'll have to eat for two, but that's never been a problem for you."

Thelma's brown eyes looked cloudy. "Miss Sally, rest her soul. She made me promise that I'd keep good food in you. I'm doing my best, but it ain't easy when you go off doing the jobs the police should be doing."

Thelma exhaled a breath and squared her shoulders. "Get

out of my kitchen. I've too much to do today for you to be wasting my time. I don't like to drive in the dark and it took me a full hour and a half to get here this morning."

Her talk continued nonstop until Fen mopped up the last bite of egg yolk with a biscuit. A text alert from Bailey came as he rose from the table.

Appt with Prissy for 9:45. Better hurry.

Chapter Fourteen

Fen reviewed a mental list of the things he knew about Priscilla Duvant as he drove, crossed over I-35, and kept going west. Prissy, as she preferred to be called, claimed to be married to Gil Duvant, the seventy-two-year-old son of Gilbert. There was some debate about their marital status that Fen needed to get clarity on.

A pause at a stoplight gave Fen a chance to look in the folder Lou had prepared for him. He read out loud. "Age: 55. Maiden name: Schwartz. Two previous marriages. Avid dog lover. Heavily involved in local animal shelter."

The light changed and the car behind him gave a two-toot honk of encouragement to get him going. He followed Williams Drive until his onboard computer told him to turn left into a newer-looking housing development. The homes looked to be of the upper-middle-class variety, with large, well-manicured lots and mostly newer cars in the driveways.

He wheeled his truck into the driveway and took stock of the ranch-style home. It would have fit in well with the rest of the neighborhood if it hadn't been for the expanse of yard signs encouraging voters to support an array of political candidates. He didn't know what to make of the biggest sign in her yard, which read *Support a Pet Cemetery in Williamson County.*

Fen left his Stetson in the truck and approached the front door. An eruption of barks came from the house as soon as his boot touched the front porch. It wasn't just one dog but an entire pack that voiced their opposition to a stranger invading their property. There was no need to ring the doorbell as a woman cracked open the solid door. He was grateful the storm door was of good quality with a secure latch. If not, two or three of the mutts might have dined on his legs.

"Stay here," shouted the woman behind the dogs. "I'll put the ones that might bite in the backyard."

He gave an enthusiastic nod and used the time to go back to his truck to grab a sketch pad and a pack of artist pencils. The pencils went into the pocket of his jacket.

In a few minutes, only two dogs accompanied the woman as she unlatched the storm door liberally decorated with paw prints. "You must be Fen, or do you prefer me to call you Sheriff Maguire?"

"Fen will do. You must be Prissy."

"I absolutely refuse to answer to any other name," she said as she led the way into a spacious living area. "It's silly to use formality between humans. We don't do the same with our pets, do we?"

He chose a chair facing the sofa and sat. "I've never thought of it that way. Thanks for seeing me, Prissy."

A brown and white dog with color-mismatched eyes and a small dog that resembled an oversized cotton ball flanked Prissy. Fen offered what he hoped they would interpret as a smile of friendship to the duo. "Good morning, puppies. You're both looking dapper today."

He shifted his gaze to Prissy. "I know the toffee-colored one is a shepherd of some sort."

"That's Donovan. He's an Australian Shepherd. The other is Adonis. He's a Bichon Frise." Prissy lowered her voice. "Please don't tell Adonis how handsome he is. Donovan's ego needs nurturing, and Adonis has a tendency to brag."

Fen looked down at the scruffier of the two. "Maybe I can help with how Donovan feels about himself. Is it all right if I make a sketch of him?"

"Sure," she replied. She tilted her head and narrowed her eyes. "I'm a bit confused. Ren was talking so fast I couldn't keep up with her. She's a living doll, but did she exaggerate about your credentials? Are you a sheriff or an artist?"

Fen spoke as he flipped open the sketch pad to a blank page. "I'm a full-time artist and former sheriff. Occasionally, I try to help law enforcement solve crimes that present unusual circumstances. That's what brings me to Georgetown. Gilbert Duvant's death." Fen cast his gaze down to the Australian Shepherd. "Along with the death of Billy, Gilbert's dog."

"Don't use that name," said Prissy with emphasis. "Donovan is very sensitive. He and you-know-who were great friends. I used to take him to the ranch for play days."

"Of course. Sorry. I understand Gilbert and his d-o-g were very close."

"They were absolutely inseparable."

A long pause followed before Fen said, "Sorry. I get lost when I'm sketching or painting. It was in the press that they found human remains on your ex-husband's property yesterday."

Prissy looked out the window to the backyard. "Gil and I are still married in the eyes of the law, and I rarely watch the news."

Fen pressed on. "There's a possibility the remains are those of your father-in-law. If you don't mind me asking, if you're still married, don't you have a claim to the estate?"

Prissy threw her head back and exploded in laughter, which lasted the better part of fifteen seconds. She brought her emotions under control and said, "Please forgive me, but Gilbert never recognized our marriage and left everything to Gil."

Fen tilted his head. "Did you contest the will?"

"Not really. Gil is an impetuous man who grew tired of wife number two and latched on to me. He offered a comfortable life with few demands other than frequent intimacy. His divorce wasn't exactly final when he moved me in with him."

She issued a coy smile. "Thank you for not reacting with scorn. I've been a free spirit all my life and I'm a hopeless lover of animals. I take my cues from the animal kingdom about so-called morality. Many people do, but they won't admit it. Take Gil, for example. We cohabitated happily for ten years until a shorter skirt caught his eyes. I was out, and she was in."

Fen stopped his sketching and looked around the living room. "I thought you went through divorce proceedings."

"We started to," said Prissy. "I told him I wanted a friendly house for my family and enough money for us to live comfortably."

"Your family?"

She pointed to the backyard. "I count all the four-legged creatures as family. I'm the mother figure to them."

Fen needed to find potential suspects, and talking to this ditsy woman wasn't getting him any closer. He kept sketching Donovan and said, "If the body turns out to be Gilbert, that means someone killed him and he didn't die in the fire. Who do you think might have wanted to harm him?"

Adonis jumped into her lap and she stroked his cotton-ball head. "I don't like to think negative thoughts like that."

Despite what she said, Fen waited to see if she would answer his question. It didn't take too long. "Gilbert made many enemies, and some of them came from under his own roof. He and Gil didn't always see eye to eye. Chance and Les, Gil's two oldest sons, are my age and are waiting like vultures for a fat inheritance."

"What about Ren's father, Robert?"

"He's so deep into the Austin music scene that he's not really in the picture."

The information went into mental file folders. Possible suspects were stacking up like wood for the fireplace. He thought there might be more.

"What about Gil's first two wives? Are they still in the picture?"

Prissy shook her head with certainty. "They're both long gone. The first bore him all three boys. The divorce was messy and expensive. To make a long story short, Gil bought and paid for his three sons to stay in the county and for Jill to leave."

Fen tried not to react but the lifting of his eyebrows gave him away.

Prissy wagged an index finger at him. "It wasn't as bad as it sounds. They didn't split until the two eldest were grown and Robert was finishing high school. Jill moved to Hawaii."

"What about wife number two?"

"That would be Anna. Gil had the money, but Anna brought sophistication into the marriage. He's an interesting blend of cowboy and businessman. She taught him how to dress for success and ground off some of the rough edges, but he was too big of a project for her and she didn't last long. She was over twenty years younger than him and couldn't see herself growing old on a ranch."

"Do you know what brought on their divorce?"

"Doomed from the start. Too much leather from him and

too much lace on her." She paused. "Perhaps it was more a case of not enough lace often enough to suit him."

Prissy threw the hand that wasn't stroking Adonis in the air. "No matter. She loved Austin, and he likes to see the horizon on the ranch. Anna talked Gil into buying a high-rise condo in Austin. It wasn't long before she was living there full-time. That left Gil alone in Williamson County. He likes dogs and younger women. I adore dogs and like older men. We both got what we wanted."

Fen asked, "There were no hard feelings when you went your separate ways?"

"It was a pleasant run while it lasted. I knew a younger woman would come along someday. It's the way of nature."

Fen tilted his head. "You're not at all bitter about splitting up?"

"Remember, I act upon animal instincts more than human feelings." She swept her hand as if she were a salesperson showing the living room on a home tour. "I traded intimacy with Gil for a pleasant home and support for my family." She looked down at her two 'sons,' whose tails wagged as she said, "Isn't that right, you two handsome boys?"

Fen put the final touches on his pencil portrait of Donovan and held up the sketch pad for inspection.

Prissy squealed with delight until Adonis snarled, barked, and whimpered.

Prissy took the sketch pad and inspected the drawing with intensity. "This is absolutely precious. Ren said you were a wonderful artist, but I never expected something like this."

Adonis, however, continued to growl and bark.

"Oh, dear. Now we've upset Adonis. Perhaps you could hold on to this until you capture Adonis' beautiful face. I'll be glad to pay you."

"Speaking with me is all the payment required," said Fen as

he stood. "I may be busy for a few days, but I'll have more questions for you if it's determined the body found is Gil's father. When I come back, I'll sketch Adonis."

The door closed behind Fen as he made his way to the driveway, not knowing what to make of Prissy. He backed onto the street, pointed his truck out of the subdivision, then pulled into a shopping center to make a call. It rang twice before Lou answered. "Before you say anything, I'm sorry for the way I acted this morning. I know Thelma means well, but she can be so intense early in the morning."

"She'll be cooking all day and then going home."

"Do you think she'd blow up if I asked her to fix me something for lunch?"

"Do it at your own risk."

"I'll grab a sandwich somewhere else and give her space."

Fen hadn't expected Lou's willingness to make amends, but he welcomed it. While he was on a roll, he needed her to confirm some things Prissy had claimed. He told her to check and double-check for a marriage license between Gil and Prissy. Also, he wanted verification if a divorce decree existed.

Lou asked, "Do you think it was a common-law marriage?"

"It could be." An idea came to him. "After you do a thorough search, call Chuck and explain what you found. Common-law marriages can be legal quicksand."

"I don't see how this case could involve Prissy."

"You're probably right, but it's an itch I need to scratch."

"Check for fleas. From the way Ren described Prissy, there's no shortage of dogs at her home."

Instead of responding to her dig, Fen said, "I'm going to the Duvant ranch and check on Bailey and Ren. After that, I'll be painting the San Gabriel. That will help me formulate a plan."

Chapter Fifteen

The trip east of town took Fen past Southwestern University, a small liberal arts institution founded by the Methodists. The diesel engine hummed as he kept a leisurely pace, never exceeding fifty-five miles an hour even though several vehicles passed him driving much faster. Signs warned of back-to-back ninety-degree turns, so he slowed to the suggested speed. He wondered how many accidents this serpentine stretch of highway had to its credit.

Fields of bottom-land marked the north river bank, while the south bank rose sharply. The more fertile side boasted pecan orchards, winter wheat, and rows of corn no more than a foot high. This was the Blackland Prairie side of Georgetown. Housing developments hadn't yet taken over. *Land For Sale* signs, however, dotted the landscape and convinced him that change was coming.

The entrance to the Duvant ranch had an automatic gate with a keypad on a pole. Asphalt played out once he went over a cattle guard. He'd learned from Ren that a light-sensitive device also controlled the gate. From daylight until dark, the gate remained open.

There wasn't another vehicle in sight, so he followed a gravel road to the old homestead of Gilbert Duvant, which was now only a scar on the land. Bailey's truck stood near the spot of the former farmhouse. He parked perpendicular to it, cut off the engine, and climbed out. Instead of rushing to where Bailey had her easel set up, he stopped and took in a full breath of country air. It made him thankful he could step out of his home back in Newman County and experience a similar earthy freshness.

Fen made a wide loop around Ren, who was engrossed in making a sketch. Instead of the bouncy young woman from yesterday, her feet looked anchored to the ground. White earbuds hung in her ears like plastic earrings. She was in an artist's zone where only the work in front of her registered. He hoped he would experience the same level of concentration later in the day. It was a secret weapon in helping him solve murders.

Bailey was a different story. She stood some distance away, facing the opposite direction, which was toward the river. She was the first to speak but made sure she whispered. "You found us."

He replied with a nod before whispering. "Are you making progress?"

"Not much. I'm having to use photos to remember the scene. I'll pack up in a little while and go back to the area where we discovered the body. There's a place where the creek meets the river that will make an awesome painting. Do you know if they took down the police tape?"

"It's likely they didn't."

"Oh well, I won't tell if you won't."

Fen shook his head but didn't chastise her. Bailey grew up

bending rules and laws, so this wasn't out of the ordinary. Since the police had plenty of time to complete their work, and the tape might be down, he didn't press the issue. Better to save a lecture for something more important.

Bailey cast her gaze at Ren. "She's seriously in flow state. Now and then she'll stop and cry."

The sound of an approaching pickup truck cut their conversation short. Fen watched the late model vehicle but spoke to Bailey. "Keep working. Your sketch is interesting."

Fen was standing beside his truck by the time the visitor arrived. Gil stepped down from his truck and whistled to the blue heeler dog that rode in the bed. The dog launched from the truck and came to the man's side, where he received a pat on the head and a hand motion for him to explore the immediate area and take care of any personal business.

He was a distinguished-looking man with gray hair protruding from under a buff-colored cowboy hat. He wore a dark suit with enough of a yoke to identify it as cowboy cut. Gil wasn't smiling. "I see you're here with Ren."

"Yes, sir. Good to see you again." Fen pointed. "The other artist is my protégé, Bailey Madison."

This placated Gil enough to extend a hand for Fen to shake.

"I was here yesterday after these two young ladies stumbled upon the body. They were looking for an interesting place to paint the river."

"Sheriff Rhoads told me. He also mentioned you have a nice spread in Newman County."

Fen's hand swept over the horizon. "It's not as big as this, but it fronts the Brazos and has good bottom land."

"I hear it has oil on it."

"A few wells."

Gil issued a soft huff through his nose. "Yeah, and I have a few head of cattle."

It was the verbal dance of cattlemen and large landowners, a sort of spitting contest to compare wealth without revealing specifics. Fen could play the game if he had to but didn't like it.

Gil squinted one eye as he looked at Fen. "Want to take a ride and look at the spread? I need to pick your brain on a thing or two."

Fen was thankful the Duvant patriarch seemed less combative today than their first meeting. "I have nothing but time today."

Gil whistled, and his dog came running at top speed. He lowered the tailgate on his truck to receive the leaping pooch, who received a word of praise.

The drive was an unhurried trip, with the first fifteen minutes taken up with talk of cattle, crops, and weather. They drove by pasture after pasture of Black Angus cattle that were fat, sleek, and too numerous to count. Even though they were just now coming out of winter, calves abounded and occasionally kicked up their heels in appreciation of the sun and green sprigs of grass.

The last question regarding wealth came from Gil when he said, "I understand you're a famous artist."

"I'd say I'm more of a lucky one. A newspaper reporter heard of me when I was a state trooper. She wrote an article because I was such an oddity. It must have been a slow news cycle because The Associated Press picked up the story. Things snowballed from there. Soon after, I stopped a bullet with my knee and had plenty of time to paint. The commissions built our home."

"Doesn't sound like luck to me. More like you were already doing two jobs." He shot Fen a quick glance. "I admire a man who doesn't sit around and wait for money to fall from the sky."

Fen tested him. "I have the impression that you wouldn't recognize any of my works if you saw them."

This earned a weak smile. "You got me on that one. The last art I looked at with any interest was in a comic book when I was a kid." His smile grew. "No offense."

"None taken, but how did you hear I'm an artist?"

"Sunny came out last night. I believe you met her at the Monument Cafe."

The gears in Fen's brain meshed. "That's right. It's hard to forget someone with a name like Sunny Day. We're renting a short-term rental from her near downtown."

"It's not hers. It belongs to a weasel named Bart Hill. Keep your hand on your wallet if you're ever around him."

"He wants to show my art in a gallery downtown."

"You might be safe doing that, but don't be surprised if he tries to get you to invest in something."

"Thanks for the warning." He took in a deep breath. "And speaking of warnings, detectives will be taking a hard look at you and your family if the body turns out to belong to your father."

"You're too late. That's where I've been since eight o'clock this morning." The words came out like the snap of a Doberman going after an intruder.

Fen allowed the squall inside the truck to pass before he softened his voice and said, "You'll be with good company. Your sons should be next."

Gil looked like he needed to spit something distasteful out of his mouth. Fen cut him off. "The cops may not say it, but they're working on the assumption that the body belongs to your father and someone murdered him."

"I figured that out about thirty seconds into the interview." He puffed out his cheeks and blew. "Any suggestions?"

"Do you have an airtight alibi?"

"Yeah, but I don't want to use it."

"You may have to."

"I was in town all night."

"I take it you weren't alone. If push comes to shove, will she corroborate your story?"

"She wouldn't want to, but she would if pressed."

Fen took in Gil's statements then had one more question. "Did you tell the detectives about her today?"

"They asked, but I told 'em I was with someone else. I know she'll vouch for me even though I wasn't with her that night."

An old rhyme came to Fen's remembrance. *Oh, what a tangled web we weave, when first we practice to deceive.* He softened the message, but not much. "Trying to outsmart the police isn't a wise strategy."

They drove in silence until Gil spoke. "You said they'd want to talk to my sons. They can rule out Robert, Ren's father. I don't think he's been in Williamson County since he flunked out of college, which only took two semesters."

"I understand he lives in Austin. That's a short drive."

"Short, but it takes a long time during rush hour or if there's a wreck on I-35. Gauging by his reluctance to visit me, you'd think it was an eight-hour drive." Gil took a breath. "Besides, that boy is weak in every way imaginable. Weak physically, emotionally, and too lazy to pick up anything but a guitar. Forget about him getting his hands dirty digging a grave, let alone having the grit to kill someone."

"What about the other two?"

"Chance is the oldest, and he lives here on the ranch. He's a full-grown man and acts like it. Dad and I marked him pretty good. Ranching is in his blood. There's a wide streak of respect for elders in him, too. He and Dad saw eye-to-eye on just about everything. He'd never raise his voice, let alone harm his grandpa."

Pride seemed to infuse every word Gil spoke about his eldest son, so Fen moved on. "What about your middle son?"

Gil's facial expression and mood changed like an unwelcome late frost nipping tomato blooms. "Let me try to explain the difference between Chance and Les. His full name is Lester, but everyone calls him Less with a double *s*. It describes him perfectly. He's fallen short of anything he's ever tried. He has some sort of worthless job working for the city."

"How was his relationship with your father?"

"Dad called him a cull." He shot a glance at Fen. "He's not completely worthless like Robert. Les leads a quiet, boring life, living paycheck to paycheck. He's so heavenly minded he's not much earthly good."

Fen was getting a good read on Gil but wanted to verify his opinion of him. "Ren is an interesting young woman. She spent the night with us last night. I hope that's all right with her family."

"That girl doesn't have sense enough to come in out of the rain, but I can't help but love her."

They'd arrived back at the site of the young artists. Fen asked, "Do you know if the deputies took down the police tape?"

"They had all night and this morning to do what they needed. I told Chance to have it down by ten o'clock this morning. Why do you ask?"

"Bailey wants to paint where the creek runs into the river."

"Is she any good?"

Fen smiled. "She'll be as good as, or better, than me someday. She's earning her way, paid off her truck, and banks a fair amount."

Gil nodded his approval. "Tell her to paint wherever she

wants." After they shook hands, the millionaire rancher-entrepreneur wasted no time leaving.

Fen walked slowly toward Bailey. He'd learned a lot, but his mind was awash with questions yet to be answered. Did Gil hurry his father's death so he could control the land? Was Gil still common-law married to Prissy? Why wasn't Billy found in the grave with the human remains? Who had a motive besides Gil?

He concluded there was much work to be done, but he needed to process what he had and hear from Lou before he interviewed anyone else. It was time to get alone, paint, and allow his mind the freedom to make sense of it.

Chapter Sixteen

F en was one hour into his painting of the river when a truck parked close to him. Too close. The driver left the diesel engine running, which was an unwelcome amount of noise. A quick glance showed the man sitting in the truck with a cell phone pressed to his ear. The distance between the truck and the easel was about ten yards.

Fen kept making light marks in pencil on the canvas. He questioned his choice of spots to paint, as this was proving to be much too popular a location. Perhaps he should have followed Bailey's lead and stayed on Duvant land. To move, or not to move? It was more likely he'd stay. After all, the location told good stories to his artist's mind.

The door to the truck slammed and the man stomped across the short distance. "We meet again, Mr. Maguire."

"Just call me me Fen, Chance."

"I'll stick with Mr. Maguire."

The man stood with thumbs hooked into the front pockets of his jeans and rocked back and forward on the heels and soles of scuffed cowboy boots. He wore a sweat-stained felt cowboy hat and a long-sleeved shirt with western yokes at the pockets and snaps instead of buttons.

"What can I do for you?"

"You can stay off Duvant land and take that smart-mouthed girl with you."

"Which one? Bailey or your niece?" asked Fen, knowing it would aggravate the surly man.

"Both, and don't get smart with me."

"I already told you that your father gave us permission to be there." Fen pointed to the man's clattering pickup. "You don't need to pretend you didn't already know that. I'll wager you were speaking with Gil just now."

The man ground his molars but didn't dispute Fen's claim to have permission. "Isn't it bad enough that you're not letting the dead rest in peace?"

Fen answered the question with one of his own. "Don't you want to see the person who killed your grandfather brought to justice?"

"By you?"

"I'm working with the sheriff."

Chance let out a huff of disgust. "For what we pay in taxes, Stony should have done the job right six months ago."

Fen knew the man had a point but didn't want to agree with him. At least not yet. "That's looking in the rearview mirror." Fen stuck his pencil in the pocket of his shirt. "You may not realize it, but we both want the same thing. To find the person responsible for killing your grandfather."

"Then why are you standing on the banks of the San Gabriel painting a stupid picture?"

"I've already conducted two interviews today, and I was processing what I learned. I have an associate at the court-house looking into county records. That smart-mouth girl you riled up was finding out all she can from Ren, and now that you're here, I'm conducting my third interview of the day."

"Huh?"

"Family and friends commit most murders. I'm wondering why you're trying to run me off when I'm not on your property. That leads me to believe that detectives talked to you today and you didn't like it."

Chance pressed his lips into a thin line but didn't answer.

"Just as I thought," said Fen. "They worked you into a lather, and you tried to take your anger out on Bailey. She's not one to be pushed around and told you to jump in the river. That made you even madder, and you came here to give me a large piece of your mind."

Chance took his thumbs out of the pockets of the jeans. "Are you accusing me of killing Grandpa?"

"Did you?"

"No!"

"Then I'm not accusing you." He paused. "That doesn't mean I won't do so in the future." He took another breath. "If it's any consolation, I don't believe you did."

"The cops do. They all but accused me of it."

Fen flipped the words away. "You'd know it if they really believed you were guilty. Don't worry until they pull out handcuffs, tell you to put your hands behind your back, and read your rights to you."

"You sound like you've had plenty of experience with this sort of thing."

"Enough to expect family members to react like you are." Fen looked toward the river. "Your grandpa shouldn't have died, but it looks like murder and someone has to pay for it."

"Are you sure it wasn't an accident?"

"I'll answer your question with one of my own. Was there anyone who pressed for it to be declared an accident?"

Chance pushed his hat up, revealing a wide forehead and thick locks of salt-and-pepper hair. "Now that you mention it, the gas company had experts on the scene pretty darn quick. They blamed the gas buildup in the house on either negligence on Grandpa's part or a faulty stove. I don't see how they could tell with the amount of destruction."

Fen thought of something else for Lou to check on. Then he realized Chance might have the information he was looking for. "Did your father pursue a civil action against the gas company?"

Chance gave his head a nod. "Dad's lawyers worked out a settlement. I'm not sure of the dollar amount. There are lots of things he doesn't tell me."

The revelation of Gil profiting even more from his father's death sent Fen's mind into overdrive. It would be most unusual for a son in his early seventies to kill his father, but money, power, and control did strange things to people.

Chance pulled his hat back down, a non-verbal sign that the conversation was over. He said something inconsequential about needing to get calves gathered for inoculations and retraced his steps back to his truck. Fen listened to the clatter of the diesel as he stood alone in front of his canvas. He had plenty to think about, and more would come tonight when Lou gave him her report.

THE SUN HUNG low on the horizon when Fen packed his easel and canvas. He considered traveling back onto Duvant land to make sure Bailey and Ren had left. Instead, he headed into town. The two young women were on their own schedule and he had his. Like homing pigeons, they'd all make it back to the rental in due time.

He was passing the university when his thoughts shifted to Thelma. His first thought was one of gratitude for her willingness to fulfill Sally's instructions that she keep him well-fed, in clean clothes, and the home ready for company. And speaking of well-fed, that chore was rapidly moving up on his list of priorities.

Thelma's car was gone by the time he parked his truck on the street. Bailey's truck and Lou's Camry occupied the driveway. They'd both beat him home. He was thankful he hadn't wasted time tracking down the two artists.

Dishes, silverware, and paper napkins were already on the table when Fen turned the corner from the living room. Bailey settled two glasses filled with amber liquid by the plates and cast a gaze his way. "Another minute or two and we'd have started without you."

"Is that fried chicken I'm smelling?" asked Fen.

Bailey shook her head. "Fried chicken is what you buy at a convenience store. This is Thelma's secret recipe, black skillet, fried chicken with mashed potatoes, gravy, green beans with chunks of ham, and apple pie for dessert."

Lou spoke loud enough to be heard from the kitchen. "You don't deserve her, Fen. I'm going to steal her away from you after I win the lottery."

Following the meal, everyone but Ren looked pleasantly miserable from gorging themselves. Bailey was the first to give words to her physical condition. "No breakfast for me tomorrow morning."

Unlike the lethargic other three, Ren sprang from her chair. "I call dibs on washing dishes."

Bailey moaned and didn't move. Neither did Lou.

Fen motioned with his head for Lou and Bailey to follow him to the living room. Ren was already singing an upbeat song as water flowed into the sink.

Once seated, Fen nodded to Lou. "How did your search of records go?"

Lou gave a snort of disappointment. "Looking for things that don't exist isn't my idea of a fun job. There's no record of either a marriage or a divorce between Gil Duvant and Priscilla, AKA Prissy. After two hours of searching, I started eavesdropping on the clerks' conversations. It didn't take long before I had the biggest gossip picked out."

Fen could picture the scene in his mind. It seemed every county office had at least one person who couldn't help but share what they knew and what they suspected. It was almost like an unwritten rule that required at least one per office. He asked, "What did you learn about Prissy and Gil?"

Lou examined her fingernails as she spoke. "It's a variation of the all-too-familiar story of a wealthy man trading in his wife and cars for newer models. Prissy had the looks and, according to my unnamed source, was a very accommodating woman. She kept a small house for appearances, but her menagerie of dogs lived at the Duvant ranch."

Bailey spoke before Fen could. "That sounds like a common-law marriage to me."

"That might be enough," said Fen. He tilted his head. "Then again, it might not."

Bailey wagged her head. "The more you talk about legal stuff, the more I'm convinced the laws can say one thing and mean something else. Do they train lawyers to think like that?"

Lou chimed in. "You're wise beyond your years."

"What else did you find out about either of them?"

"Believe it or not, Prissy remains true to Gil, even though he and Sunny are the hot item of conversation around town. The old millionaire and young business woman have frequent *business lunches* together." Lou put air quotes around *business lunches.*

"I also learned that Prissy is ga-ga about dogs. Unfortunately for her, the people in positions of power don't agree with her that the most pressing need in the county is a pet cemetery."

"Why doesn't Gil peel off a few acres from that huge ranch and give it to her?" asked Bailey.

Fen took a stab at the answer. "The way people think about pets has radically changed over the years. You can see the difference in the words *owner* and *caregiver*. I'll bet you anything Gil's father taught him that dogs were welcome if they performed a useful function on the ranch. I saw it in his face today when he petted his blue heeler. It's a shepherding dog and not a bad guard dog all rolled up into one. He can help round up cattle, warn of snakes or coyotes, and live on table scraps. On winter nights, dogs used to keep their masters warm. Ever heard of a three-dog night?"

"Weren't they an old rock group?"

Lou expelled a huff. "You sure know how to make me feel old."

Fen explained. "A three-dog night was one that was so cold it took three dogs in bed with you to keep you warm."

Lou interrupted. "Before you ask, I found nothing of significance about any of the other family members. Chance was married once but had no children. He married a woman seven years his junior and divorced after twelve years. My source told me Chance blamed his wife because she couldn't give him an heir after multiple rounds of in-vitro failed."

"Creep," said Bailey.

Fen settled deeper into the chair. "That also wasn't unusual in days gone by, except wealthy men, in various cultures, took a shortcut and had their infertile wives killed so they could produce an heir by another wife."

Lou added, "Other cultures found a work-around by practicing polygamy."

"Yuk."

Fen smiled at Bailey's response. He leaned forward and lowered his voice. "Do you have anything to contribute to the investigation?"

She looked toward the dining room that Ren would have to walk through to get to the living room. Her words were barely audible. "I'm taking it slow with her. Tomorrow afternoon we're going to Austin to visit her parents. Her dad doesn't get up before two or three."

"I may want to go with you."

The sound of Ren's phone ringing came as their conversation lagged. All three listened as if they might catch a word or two. They didn't.

It was rare to see a look of worry darken Ren's countenance. She blurted out, "Cory just called me. Grandpa Gil's hurt bad. He didn't make that first sharp curve coming into town. The ambulance isn't there yet. I need to go."

"We all do," said Fen. "You three go to the hospital. I'm going to the site of the crash."

Chapter Seventeen

The hurried ride to the crash site was all too familiar. How many times had Fen heard the police dispatcher call out his badge number and tell him to respond to yet another 10-50 major? That was police jargon for a vehicle-involved incident with injuries. The only difference this time was the report came from a free-spirited young woman with a friend who was a deputy and the injured person was Ren's grandfather.

A deputy sheriff's SUV sat blocking traffic at a crossroads with lights punching blue and red holes in the night sky. Fen realized he'd need to bluff his way past the deputy if he were to have any chance of examining the cause of the crash. He pulled off the road to the right and stepped out. It was a welcome surprise to see Deputy Cory Blane.

"The road's blocked," hollered Cory. "You need to go around."

Fen closed the distance until Cory said, "Oh, it's you, Sheriff Maguire. There's been an accident."

"I know, Ren told me."

Cory faced oncoming traffic and waved them away with his flashlight pointing to a county road. After the driver pulled a quick U-turn, Cory refocused. "I hope Ren didn't tell anyone else."

"Just Bailey and another lady who's helping me with the case." Fen looked into the distance but couldn't see emergency lights. "Do you know if the sheriff's coming?"

"He should be here any minute." Cory spotted another vehicle coming, but it was a long way off. "This is the first time I've heard of him responding to a 10-50. It must have something to do with the murder case."

"It might. That's what I'm hoping to find out."

"That's good enough for me. We've been told to do what we can to help you find who killed old man Duvant." He paused. "Not everyone is happy about it. They believe you're stepping on their turf, if you know what I mean."

"I do, and it doesn't surprise me. I'll be sure not to mention your name if I'm asked how I knew to come here."

"Thanks. I'm learning there's a lot they didn't teach me. Internal politics isn't my thing, but I guess it's part of the job."

"Like walking on a tightrope, isn't it?"

A nod answered the question.

Fen retreated to his truck and made a quick getaway, waving at Cory as he passed. It wasn't long before emergency lights appeared in the distance. He passed the first ninety-degree turn and looked for a place to park before he came to the second. A farmhouse gave him a place to turn around and park with his truck pointed back to town. From there, he closed the distance to the emergency vehicles on foot.

The first person he approached was a state highway patrolman with chevrons on his sleeve. They recognized each other, which served the purpose of Fen not having to explain himself to others. As they conversed, an unmarked vehicle sped toward them and came to a quick stop behind the sergeant's car. Out stepped Sheriff Rhoads.

"I should have known you'd beat me here," said Stony. "You must still have a police band radio in your truck."

Fen neither confirmed nor denied the statement. Instead, he said, "Hope you don't mind if I look at Gil's truck."

"That's why I came, too. Let's check it out."

"It rolled at least twice," said the state trooper. "Air-bags deployed and he was wearing a seat belt. Otherwise, we'd be working a fatality."

Fen and Stony made a stop at the ambulance. The sheriff approached a man with muscular tattooed arms who wore the T-shirt of an EMT. Stony made a quick inquiry. "Is he going to make it?"

Fen inspected the tattoos with more diligence. They told the story of military service as a combat medic.

"He should, unless his internal injuries are worse than expected or he has a bleeder in the brain. He'll be alive when they get him to the hospital."

The sheriff nodded. He and Fen walked on while Stony asked, "Did you hear what the state trooper said about Gil wearing his seat belt?"

"Yeah. Is that important?"

"Out of character. He grew up driving pickups without shoulder restraints and shoved the lap belt into the gap between the seat's bottom and back. He told me he'd rather pay an attorney to beat a ticket than drive with one."

"My farm manager thinks the same thing. He says cars and trucks run on horsepower. He'll wear a seatbelt when they put 'em on saddles."

This earned a smile. The condition of the truck took the

smile away. It stood on its wheels but looked like a mighty hand had mashed down on the top. The front bumper lay by itself some distance away. The ground around the truck was littered with discarded wrappings of medical supplies. Dirt, mud, and dents completed the scene of destruction.

Fen and the sheriff both carried flashlights as they approached a deputy with a lieutenant bar on each collar. A second man wearing street clothes was shining his flashlight inside the cab of the truck.

The sheriff took care of introductions. The man in slacks and a blue shirt bore the title of detective. Stony added context that this was the man heading up the reopened inquiry into Gilbert Duvant's death.

The detective gave Fen a narrow-eyed, quick inspection and looked to his boss. "It looks to me like the corner tried to kill another person. The short skid marks tell me he was speeding going into the corner. He didn't apply brakes until it was too late."

Fen moved away as the detective waxed on about how many injuries and fatalities the corner had claimed over the years he'd been on the force. With flashlight in hand, Fen moved to look at the blood-stained interior. The driver's door yawned open, which allowed him to see someone had cut the seat belt. This gave first responders quick access to extract the body. He slowly walked around the exterior, searching for something in particular which he didn't find.

When he returned to the driver's side, he pulled a red bandanna from his back pocket. The crumpled roof support beam was his target. He theorized the mud-caked beam had gone through a wet spot on one of its flips. He used the bandanna to scrape off the mud.

"Stony," said Fen. "You'd better look at this."

Stony, the detective, and the lieutenant took quick steps to where Fen stood with his flashlight illuminating the length of crumpled metal. "What does that look like to you?" asked Fen.

"Let me see that rag," demanded the detective. He cleaned off the area even more and took a step back.

The sheriff took his place. "It looks to me like we have an attempted murder and not an accident."

He spun around and stared at the detective. "This is the second time you've been too quick to declare a serious crime an accident. Be waiting for me outside my office tomorrow morning. Go home."

The lieutenant took the sheriff's place and examined the shiny round hole that had pierced the metal of the support beam. He turned to Fen. "How did you know where to look?"

The sheriff scowled at his lieutenant. "A better question to ask is why you didn't think to look for it. I suggest you get a bottle of water, wash off any mud on the exterior, and look for additional bullet holes. I want the round that made this one found, and I don't care how long it takes or what you have to do to find it."

It was time for Fen to make a tactical retreat. He'd found what he suspected and inadvertently took away any lingering doubts that Williamson County had one homicide and one attempted killing, all involving the same family. A house fire hadn't taken the life of the patriarch, and the surviving heir hadn't had a tragic accident. The ambulance sped toward town.

The trip to the hospital gave Fen time to ponder how full the day had been, and it wasn't over yet. He'd spoken with three people whom he'd placed on a list as suspects. One of them was now a victim, and instead of moving closer to the responsible party, he sensed the investigation slipping from his grasp.

A thought occurred to him as he drove past the university. Who would come to the hospital to check on Gil's condition? Another question followed quickly. How would they react to the news that Gil survived? A third question marched in on the heels of the last. How would they react if he died?

Chapter Eighteen

The lights in the emergency waiting area seemed unusually bright as Fen passed through the automatic doors that whooshed open. He was suddenly reminded of all the long days he spent at the hospital with Sally. Now he generally avoided hospitals if at all possible.

Bailey was on her feet. "They won't tell us anything. The last we heard, Gil's here, and we're not to bother the staff. Lou didn't like that answer. She's looking for someone who can tell her something. What do you know?"

Fen looked at a chair away from other visitors. Ren sat with knees touching her chest. Her arms clasped so tightly around her legs that she looked like a ball with a head attached. She stared into space and rocked back and forth.

"Go get her," said Fen. "We'll take her outside and I'll tell you two what I know."

Bailey spun and retrieved the young woman with frayed emotions. Fen hoped what he had to say wouldn't send her over the edge.

The group went some twenty yards down a sidewalk after

they cleared the door. Fen cast his gaze to each young woman but settled it on Ren. "A paramedic told me he believed your grandpa will make it."

Ren reacted to the news with a weak nod. "That means he might not."

Fen made his best attempt to put hope into his next words. "The man knows his business, but he didn't pull any punches. I believe your grandpa is a man who won't allow himself to die until he's good and ready. Right now, they're doing everything possible by running all kinds of tests to determine the extent of his injuries. I know it's hard to take, but the longer we hear nothing, the better the news is likely to be."

Ren shook her head at this. "All these negative vibes are doing weird things to me. I feel like I need to go someplace and melt."

"That's normal."

"I bet you never melted."

"He has," said Bailey. "We both have."

"Really?"

Both nodded.

Bailey took a step back. "Letting all those feelings out won't make it go away, but it helps. I've had a lot of practice dealing with my emotions. For years, I wanted to go home and sleep in my old bed and have my daddy tuck me in. I couldn't because he died."

"You're going through an enormous shock," said Fen. "Have you called your parents?"

"Not yet. Dad should be at a club by now. I don't know if Mom went with him tonight or not."

Bailey gave her a nod of encouragement and teasingly spoke as only a friend would. "Well, duh! Don't you remember how to use that phone in your back pocket?"

Ren gave her a wan smile.

Fen took a step toward the door and spoke to Bailey as he left. "Take care of Ren tonight. I have things to do."

Bailey looked at Ren. "I'll leave you alone to call your mom."

A few moments later, Fen and Lou sat side by side in a quiet corner of the waiting room.

"Spill it," whispered Lou. "What's the scoop?"

He whispered back. "It wasn't an accident."

Lou's eyes widened. "If you tell me I can't report this, I may do something we'll both regret."

"I can't give you the pictures on my phone, but here's what happened." Fen spoke in hushed tones as he relayed partial details. He described the cause of the wreck as suspicious and under investigation.

Lou interrupted him every third sentence with questions while she took notes. She looked at a clock mounted on the wall. "I know you're holding something back, but I have enough to call this in."

Fen held up a hand to stop her. "Don't use my name as your source."

Before she could ask him another probing question, Fen stood. "I'll be in the cafeteria drinking coffee. Unless I'm mistaken, we'll be here most of the night."

It came as no surprise that he'd only drained half a cup when Lou slid into the booth opposite him. He'd known the few tidbits he'd given wouldn't last her long. She was consistent in always wanting to know more.

Her words tumbled out. "Bailey was short on details and long on excitement. Ren sent her a text saying her mom's on her way." She took a breath and leaned forward. "She said something about a shooting, but the nurse I spoke with mentioned nothing about Gil being shot."

"He wasn't, but it wasn't from lack of trying. If you give me a chance to tell you without interruptions, I'll give you the full story."

Lou clamped her teeth together so hard they made an audible click. She pulled out a small recorder, turned it on, and set it on the table.

In what Fen thought was plenty of detail, he gave his account of what he'd seen and done. He should have known it wouldn't be enough to satisfy her.

"Are they sure the truck rolled two times?"

"At least two, possibly three."

"Could you tell from the bullet hole the caliber of the weapon?"

"Forensics might. It was powerful enough to rip through the metal roof support and keep going."

"Is there any chance it lodged in the vehicle?"

"Doubtful."

"Why?"

"I put myself in the shooter's place and imagined how I would take the shot. Let's say the truck is coming at me at around sixty miles an hour, but it's slowing down to about fifty to make the curve. Concealment is important. It's a cleared fence line at that corner with no trees, so I'm in a prone position."

"I get it," said Lou. "Belly on the ground."

"Correct. The land where I'd take the shot is before the curve starts. It's a little higher than the pavement but not higher than a person sitting in a pickup. That means the bullet will have a slight upward trajectory. The round struck the bottom of the roof support. It went straight through, but where did it go next? The most likely track is through the window on the passenger's side. The sheriff will have people with metal detectors looking for it at first light." Fen quickly added, "That's an educated guess on my part."

Lou processed the information with amazing speed. "What you're saying is, the shooter had two chances of killing Gil. They could have made a lucky shot or they could have intended to make it look like an accident."

"The sound of exploding metal and glass is plenty to cause any driver to miss a sharp curve."

"Which do you think is most likely?"

Fen thought for a few seconds. "The latter. I believe they'd prefer it to look like another accident. Either way, they almost accomplished their goal."

Lou turned off the recorder. "I particularly like the part of you finding the bullet hole and showing up the snooty detective. Stories of police incompetence are pure gold."

Fen lifted a hand to cut her off. "You know the rules. You report only the facts and leave the commentary to others."

Her hand vibrated with frustration.

"Remember, when you call it in, you can't use my name as a source."

"Why not?"

Fen leaned forward. "No more questions. Call in the update to your story and make it quick. I need you to go to the waiting room and watch to see who arrives and how they react. One of them will probably be the person who took a shot at Gil. Pretend you don't know me, but I'll give you a signal."

"Give me names now."

"You already have them." Fen considered a more complete answer. "Ren's mother is coming. I get the impression that her father isn't. You're the pro. Find out all you can about Robert and his wife."

"Who else?"

"Family members. Don't be surprised if politicians, business leaders, and others of influence make an appearance. They could be good filler for your stories."

She gave him a stare. "You scare me when you think like a reporter."

He had no answer for this, so he stood. "Wait until I'm gone to leave. Remember, you don't know me. For the rest of the night, you're a freelance reporter."

Fen made it back to the waiting room and settled in a chair that faced the door. His cup of coffee was down to the dregs when Prissy burst through the door carrying Adonis, her white ball of fur. She made straight for the information desk, setting her sights on a man with a full head of thick, gray hair.

"I need to see the doctor treating Gil Duvant."

The volunteer turned his head toward a computer monitor. Fen couldn't hear the man's response, but Prissy's words traveled all the way to where he sat. Most everyone in the room turned their head to take in the scene as Prissy belted out, "That's not acceptable. Get the doctor out here now!"

Additional soft tones came from the man.

Prissy's volume intensified. "Are you deaf, you old fool? I don't care what your protocol is."

Fen rose and took steps toward the information desk as Prissy railed on. She was between insults when Fen drew close enough to see the man's hospital badge with his name, photo, and VOLUNTEER on it.

"Lady, I already told you. Doctors consult with family members when they can." He then tilted his head about five degrees and asked, "Are you his wife?"

"Of course, I'm his wife."

It was after this declaration that Fen noticed Prissy had placed her petting hand behind her back and crossed her fingers.

The countenance of the volunteer morphed from an obliging grandfather to that of someone who had a limit to how they were to be treated. He pointed to the dog. "No pets allowed in the waiting area."

"He's a registered service dog. He stays with me, and I'm staying here."

The volunteer shook his head. "He's not wearing a vest with an identification tag. Even if he was, hospital policy says no pets in the ER or ER waiting area. Special arrangements have to be made with the hospital administrator for in-room visits."

Prissy exploded in a tirade of insults. The man picked up a phone.

Fen stepped forward before the man could punch in a number. "No need to call security. I'm a friend of the family. I'll take her outside and tell her what I know."

"Please, do. Make it clear to her she can't bring the dog back in."

Prissy opened her mouth to lambaste the man again, but Fen had already grabbed her arm and unceremoniously turned her toward the door. This surprised her enough to still her mouth, but not the sparks that flew from her eyes. He whispered words that changed her expression. "I came from the crash site. Once we're outside, I'll tell you what happened."

Fen spotted Bailey and Ren standing where he'd left them. Ren had her back to him so she couldn't see Fen direct Prissy an equal distance in the opposite direction. Once there, he positioned himself so he could see the young ladies in the distance and Bailey could track him.

It was a cool night and Prissy was ill-prepared for it in a paisley print garment that caught the spring breeze and billowed like a parachute. She clutched the shivering Adonis to her breast as Fen gave her most of the details of his visit to the crash site.

The news that the paramedic believed Gil wasn't likely to

die brought her emotions mostly under control. He then pretended to notice Bailey and Ren for the first time. Fen motioned with a wave and the four walked toward each other until they met outside the door.

"Bailey, this is Prissy."

"I feel like I already know you. Ren's been talking about you for two days. I hear you're the biggest dog lover in the state."

Fen broke in before Prissy could respond. The twinkle in her eye told him Bailey was well on her way to making a new friend who would talk at length about her passion for pooches.

Fen slid a positive tone into his words. "Why don't Ren and I go in and wait for news on Gil while Bailey, Prissy, and Adonis get out of this chilly air? Ren can come out and deliver updates."

Prissy gave a nod of approval and stroked Adonis. "That's acceptable, given the circumstances." She gave the pooch a kiss on his muzzle. "My baby didn't like that awful man, did you honey-bunch? Miss Bailey will come sit with us and you'll make a new friend."

The seat that gave Fen a clear view of the door was still open, as was the one next to it. They occupied them, but only for a few seconds. The doors opened and a group of six men entered.

Ren shot from her chair. "There's Uncle Les. It looks like he brought the deacons in his church with him." She took Fen by the hand. "Come meet him before the pastor and the women's prayer ministry show up."

"I'd love to," said Fen.

Chapter Nineteen

There wasn't anything special that drew one's eye to Les Duvant other than the star-shaped scar on his forehead. It was visible only when he wore his baseball cap pushed back on his forehead. The tan line told Fen that wasn't often. Perhaps it was the plainness of his dress, manner, and speech that made him instantly likable.

A firm handshake and a meeting of gazes accompanied Ren's introduction. Les spoke first. "Thanks for taking in Ren. I hope she didn't keep you up all night. The Lord gave her a double helping of words when He made her."

"It's people like Ren who bring extra flavor to life," said Fen.

Ren took her uncle's hand in hers. "That makes me a stuffed-crust pepperoni pizza with double jalapeños."

Both men chuckled and nodded in agreement.

With the ice broken, Fen needed to get Les alone to see how this middle brother fit into the Duvant family portrait. Les came to his rescue without prompting. "Ren, I need a few moments alone with Sheriff Maguire."

Ren unclasped her hand and held it with a palm toward her uncle, who gave her a high five. "I thought after my last birthday I'd get a ticket into adult conversations. I guess not."

The words were pure tongue-in-cheek. She hugged Les and spoke as she took a step toward the door. "I'm going to talk to Aunt Prissy and Bailey. Adonis may want to spend some time with me. I haven't seen him since Great-Grandpa's funeral."

Les spoke with the group of men that had arrived with him, which took all of twenty seconds. He returned and asked, "Can I buy you a cup of coffee?"

"No, thanks," said Fen. "Did you send them to the hospital's chapel?"

A single blink of surprise came as Les said, "Few people think of hospital chapels, let alone go there to pray. You're no stranger to them, are you?"

The thought of how much time he'd spent praying for his late wife as her body rejected the transplanted heart tightened his chest so he couldn't respond with anything but a quick nod.

Les took over while Fen righted his emotional ship. "Let's take a walk. There's a nice wooded area where we'll be alone."

Les carried the conversation on the way. "I knew about you losing your wife. Isn't it amazing how much you can find out about people with a simple computer search? I do that whenever Ren calls me and says she's spending the night with someone I don't know. She's sometimes too trusting for her own good."

"You're a good man for looking after her."

"She reminds me so much of a butterfly. Beautiful, harmless, and one who brings joy to people with her art and by being herself." Les paused. "Tell me about Bailey. I hear she has genuine talent. How did she come to live with you?"

"In the most unusual way. I was setting up my easel on the banks of the Brazos. Bailey's uncle floated by and his body hung up in a tree that had fallen into the water. That started a series of events where I was involved in helping solve the murder. During the investigation we were sort of thrown together, which carried on when an arsonist set fire to the trailer she lived in. She suffered a serious burn. Did you notice her left hand?"

"I saw what looked like skin grafts."

Fen continued. "The fire turned her place to live into a pile of ashes. She had no place to go after they released her from a burn center hospital in Houston. She's been living in an apartment over my garage ever since. It's big enough that she has a small studio too."

Fen realized the conversation had focused only on him and Bailey. He appreciated how easy Les was to talk to, but both men had other things on their minds. Then it occurred to him that Les hadn't inquired about his father's condition.

"I went to the crash site," said Fen as a way of turning the conversation.

"Oh?"

"The paramedic I spoke with seemed encouraged."

"Praise God."

Nothing followed, so Fen pressed on. "The truck rolled twice. They believe the airbags and seatbelt saved him."

"I'm sure that's how the official report will read and what the press will report."

Fen quirked his head to an angle. "What would you add?"

Les spoke with calm confidence as he said. "You said my father was wearing his seat belt?"

"That's right. I saw where first responders cut the webbing on the shoulder and lap belts in order to remove him. I also saw the deployed center and side airbags."

A strange smile crossed Les's face. "My father had a mechanic disconnect the warning signal to his seat belt. He's a hard man who hates government regulations. I've never known him to wear a seat belt in his life."

Fen wondered how to respond, but the words shot out before he could pull them back in. "Do you think God told him to wear his seat belt?"

"He might have, but Dad would have ignored God. It's more likely an angel fastened it for him." He paused. "I can think of one more possibility that most people would prefer. Someone Dad trusted warned him to take extra precautions."

"Any ideas who that person might be?"

Les gave a coy smile. "I'm more inclined to believe the angel theory. My natural mind came up with the idea that someone warned him." He took in a deep breath. "My father is a very wealthy and influential man. That alone makes him a man some people want to get close to and gain his favor. Others want to take from him."

Fen considered the words for long seconds before he responded. "Is Sunny Day one who's trying to gain his favor? There's a rumor that he wants to marry her."

"Ah," said Les. "You've discovered my father's weakness." He looked away, then brought his gaze back. "If they were already married, I'd suspect her of causing the wreck that has us all here tonight."

Les stuck his hands in the front pockets of his jeans. "Correct me if I'm wrong. The accident tonight wasn't an accident at all."

Fen issued a weak nod.

"I thought so." He rocked back on the heels of his work boots. "Detectives interviewed me today concerning my grandfather's death. I expect them to talk to me again about what happened tonight."

Fen nodded. "They will."

"I'm a simple man who's content to live a quiet life and

make a living with my hands, but that won't stop them from raking me over the coals."

"Why would they do that?"

Les pointed to his forehead. "If you're wondering how I got this scar, my father did this to me. He didn't like the idea that I wanted nothing to do with ranching or growing the Duvant empire. He thought it was a simple case of teenage rebellion, and the way to deal with that was to beat it out of me. His rod of discipline was a two-by-two yardstick made of hickory. He meant to hit me in the back, but I spun and bent over as he swung."

"Did your father use the same type of discipline on Chance and Robert?"

"Only a belt on Chance, and not that often. He's cut from the same cloth as my dad and was the obedient son who never left home. Robert was the baby and marched to a completely different drummer, literally and figuratively. Dad wrote Robert off as a lost cause and focused on Chance and me."

Les looked toward the front of the hospital. "There's my pastor and the other deacons. I need to get to the prayer room."

Questions flooded Fen's mind, but they'd have to wait. Les had given him plenty to process. Still, he needed to drill deeper into this well of information. "How would you like to meet me for breakfast in the next day or two?"

"I'd like that. How 'bout the day after tomorrow at Just Love Coffee?"

"You're the second person who's recommended that coffee shop to me. I hear they have good waffles."

"Good food and an even better atmosphere. They open at 6:00 a.m."

Fen was in no hurry to go back inside, so he bid farewell to Les. Under the canopy of trees, conflicting feelings assailed his mind and emotions. The cop side of his brain told him to be suspicious. So many lies had come his way in the twenty years he'd worn a badge. Was Les really uninterested in the family fortune, or was this a cagey man playing the long game to receive his cut of the inheritance if his father was out of the picture?

One thing was for sure. Les wasn't what Fen expected.

After an indeterminate time and without thinking about it, Fen ambled toward the hospital's emergency room entrance. Bailey and Prissy intercepted him as he stepped onto a sidewalk.

He looked at Prissy. "Is Ren taking care of Adonis?"

"She and her father are the only sane members of the Duvant family."

Fen countered with, "Les seemed all right to me."

"He's better than most, but I'm not into myths and legends. Besides, he's a meat-eater."

It was on Fen's mind to remind her that a host of animals were carnivores, but he refrained. Instead, he asked, "Is Ren's mother on the way?"

Bailey answered, "She's five minutes out. It helped Ren to sit in the car and hold Adonis. He's a sweet little dog."

Prissy puffed with pride. "The world would be a much better place if we respected and appreciated dogs." She looked toward the door. "Has there been any report on Gil's condition?"

"Not that I've heard," said Fen. "Let's go in and check."

Prissy led the way and went directly to the information desk. A young woman wearing hospital scrubs appeared from behind double doors that led to the treatment rooms. "Duvant family?" she announced.

Prissy strode toward her. "I'm Gil's wife. How is he?"

Fen hadn't noticed, but Sunny Day had entered the room and taken a seat while he spoke with Les. She rose and came close enough to hear but stayed behind Prissy so she couldn't see her.

The doctor wore her face mask under her chin. She directed her remarks in surprisingly loud tones to Prissy. "Mr. Duvant sustained three broken ribs in the accident. The fractures are simple, which means they don't require surgery. Otherwise, the CT scan and X-rays showed nothing of significance. He received a facial laceration and another on the scalp. A plastic surgeon was called in to close those. I've ordered him to spend the night in ICU out of an abundance of caution. He lost consciousness in the accident because of head trauma." She took a breath. "All things considered, he's a lucky man and should make a full recovery."

Fen had stationed himself so he could see Prissy and Sunny's reactions at the same time. Sunny eased closer as Prissy sought additional details from the doctor. The doctor added virtually nothing to the report, turned, and walked back to the doors where she swiped an identification badge and disappeared.

Prissy turned to face Sunny. They placed what appeared to be comforting hands on each other shoulders and exchanged whispers.

The waiting area doors swished open, and in walked Bart Hill. He scanned the room and glanced at Sunny. The eye contact lasted only a blink, but it was long enough. Instead of staying in the room, Bart went to the hallway with a sign pointing to the cafeteria.

It wasn't long before Sunny retrieved her purse and went down the same hall. Fen caught Lou's attention and nudged his head in Sunny's direction. Lou understood the non-verbal instructions to follow and try to eavesdrop.

Chapter Twenty

It was one of those days where information seemed to come like waves of heavy surf. Fen wondered how much more would roll in. Lou would hopefully overhear the conversation between Sunny and Bart. Ren's mother would arrive at any moment. Gil would survive the attempt on his life but wouldn't be available to interview for at least another day, and then only after the sheriff's detectives questioned him. Les was a bit of a wild card. Was he so much at peace that he didn't appear to be overly concerned about his father's condition, or was there something more sinister under the calm facade?

Bailey nudged him in the ribs with her elbow. "What's next?"

He came to his senses and looked down at the petite artist. He whispered, "You've spent considerable time with Ren. Have you noticed any deception?"

"Nah. Whatever pops into her mind comes out of her mouth. I'm not sure she knows how to lie."

"Good. Don't teach her. She's the best source of unfiltered

information we have." Fen started walking. "Let's go outside. I've exceeded my quota of time in a hospital."

Bailey waited until the door closed behind them before she asked, "Did I see you motion for Lou to follow that older version of a Barbie doll?"

"That's Sunny Day."

"That can't be her real name."

"Yep. Easy to remember. Unless I'm mistaken, she's meeting a man named Bart Hill in the cafeteria. He's a real mover and shaker in the county. Owns an art gallery downtown."

"He has nice hair and snappy clothes," said Bailey. "I don't trust guys like that. Do you think he could be behind Ren's grandpa's murderer?"

"No evidence, yet."

"That's not what I asked."

"Right now, the possibilities are almost too many to count."

Bailey blew out a breath of frustration. "Back to my original question. What's next?"

"I need to get Ren's mother alone and find out what I can about Ren's father."

Bailey's bottom lip stuck out. "I hope he isn't involved. I like Ren. It would break her heart."

"Don't forget," said Fen. "We go where the evidence leads us, no matter what."

The door slid open and Prissy walked by them, speaking as she passed. "That's wonderful news about Gil. He'll live to chase more short skirts. Adonis and I need to get home to the rest of the family."

Ren carried Adonis to Prissy, and the two met halfway to Prissy's Subaru. A third woman met them as Fen and Bailey watched from a distance. The woman wore the uniform of someone who worked in a corporate office—slacks, a print blouse, and a blazer. She drew Ren into her arms and gave what looked like a mother's hug.

Bailey summarized. "That can't be Ren's mom. She looks like an accountant."

"Perhaps she is," said Fen. He didn't want to admit that the woman's appearance wasn't what he expected, either. "Let's find out."

Prissy was driving away by the time Fen and Bailey approached. Ren held on to the woman's hand. "Mom, this is my new BFF, Bailey Madison, and the handsome man with her is Fen Maguire. This is my mom, June. Fen's the best artist I ever met."

The woman extended a hand. "Ren's gushed about you for two days. I hope she's not been any trouble."

"On the contrary. She and Bailey have been doing their own thing, and I've been doing mine."

"That's what I want to talk to you about," said June. "I'm not sure what to think about my daughter being involved in a murder investigation."

"I'm not," countered Ren. "Bailey and I spent the day painting."

June looked over the top of her eyeglasses that rode low on her nose. "You also discovered a body, and now we're at the hospital where your grandfather is being treated. That tells me there's more to this story than you're telling me."

June gave her daughter another piercing stare. "Do you still want to go home with me tonight?"

Ren looked down at the ground. "I did, but now I'm not so sure."

Fen broke into the conversation. "The doctor delivered a report on Gil's condition. He's out of danger with a few broken ribs, a few stitches, and a concussion. He's expected to make a full recovery."

Ren spun in a circle with arms outstretched. "Yippee! Grandpa's going to be fine. That means I can stay and finish my painting." She gulped a breath and rambled on. "Mr. Fen wanted me to paint a picture of Great-Grandpa with him and Great-Grandma dancing in the kitchen. You remember the stories Dad told about how much Great-Grandpa loved peach pie. I had to guess what they must've looked like when they were young, but I can see them clearly. It's like Mr. Fen opened up a whole new world of painting to me, and he hasn't even given me pointers yet."

June blunted any more words with upraised hands. "Your father's always wanted you to follow your dreams, but I sense danger. Mr. Maguire and I will discuss the situation and I'll determine if you stay or go home with me."

Fen looked at Bailey. "Why don't you and Ren go somewhere and get some ice cream?"

Ren wiggled her eyebrows. "I know just the place, but we need to hurry. I'm getting bubble gum flavored. They have about thirty flavors and they're all yummy, except licorice. I can't stand licorice."

Ren took off running toward Bailey's truck. "I'll beat you there."

"Yes, you will."

Fen cast his gaze to June. "Can I buy you a cup of coffee?"

"I'd prefer Chai tea."

"Let's see what they have in the cafeteria."

Fen gave an edited account of the accident, which seemed to only partially satisfy June. He then asked what kind of work she did.

"I'm an auditor for the IRS. There's a regional office in Austin."

Fen countered with a smile. "You and I have more in common than I thought."

"How's that?"

"People try to hide things from us."

This earned a weak chuckle. "You don't know the lengths people will go to in order to keep information from me. And then they blame us when the amount due isn't what they expected."

They reached the cafeteria, and June had to settle for hot water and a bag of Earl Gray tea. Fen got an obligatory cup of coffee but knew he'd not drink all of it.

June looked up from stirring some artificial sweetener into her cup. "That was a clever thing you did."

"What's that?"

"You equated my job with what you do." She looked over her glasses into his right eye. "What exactly is your job?"

"Full-time artist, part-time private investigator." He paused. "It's actually more complicated than that because I'm a former sheriff and still a certified peace officer."

"Do you arrest people?"

He shook his head. "I haven't since I retired and don't want to. Gathering information and turning it over to the cops is plenty for me."

"Do you specialize in any type of crime?"

"Homicides." He paused. "At least that's all I've worked on so far."

"You speak like it's a hobby."

Fen took the plastic lid off his paper cup to let his coffee cool. "My late wife made me promise to do something besides paint. Being an artist is a solitary life. She knew I'd spend weeks or months alone in my studio if I didn't do something else. The occasional case takes me out of my home and puts me around people again."

He took a sip from the cup and resettled it on the table.

"And speaking of gathering information about a murder, I need to pick your brain."

"That was quite a transition," said June. "I take it you believe my husband's grandfather didn't die in a house fire caused by a gas explosion."

Fen answered with a shake of his head. "Have detectives from the sheriff's department come to talk to your husband yet?"

The question didn't seem to rattle June. "Not yet, and I don't see why they would." She stared into her cup of tea. "However, your question tells me we should expect a visit."

"Probably tomorrow," said Fen. "They might have come tonight, but Gil's wreck put them behind schedule."

"I notice you didn't say Gil's accident."

Fen leaned forward. "You have excellent interviewing skills. Words have meanings, and you pay close attention to what people say."

Shadows of concern deepened the worry lines radiating from June's eyes. "Is Gil still in danger?"

"I believe he is."

June brought her hands together on the top of the table. "You've been very open and honest with me, and I appreciate it. What do you want to know?"

This was the reaction Fen had hoped for. He'd read June correctly. She listens to lies and deception so often that she could spot it if he'd tried to deceive her. Now was the time to pepper her with questions.

"Does your husband hate his father?"

"He used to, but not so much anymore. It's more like they divorced each other. There's no common ground other than the same last name."

"Does Robert expect to receive an inheritance?"

"That's not something we talk about," she said, then paused

a moment. "This may sound selfish, but I'd love to receive an inheritance. Auditing tax returns isn't my idea of what I want to do until I'm sixty-five."

"What is?"

"Being able to use my skills to help musicians manage their money. They're hopeless with credit cards and bank balances."

"Does that include your husband?"

June straightened her spine. "Robert is the type of man who spends fifty dollars for every forty he earns. He pretends not to know the difference between gross and net income. His joy comes from doing what he loves, which is playing music in Austin. He never asks what a gig will pay before he commits to it."

Fen was getting a read on the youngest of the three brothers but needed to dig deeper. "How does Robert get along with his brothers?"

"Not well with Chance. Some of it may stem from them being so far apart in age, but that's not all. Chance is old-school Duvant, but only up to a point. His passion is quality livestock. He wants the ranch to be known for the best beef in the state."

Fen asked, "Are you saying he'd be willing to let go of some land if it would help him grow higher-quality beef?"

"Not all the land is river bottom. There's some that weeds have a hard time growing on."

Fen ran a hand down his face and felt the stubble of a day's growth. "What about Gil? Is he willing to sell some of the land?"

"Not a chance," came the answer with emphasis. "He'd be afraid his father would come back from the dead and put a scar on his head like the one he gave Les. Besides, Gil made more money in shrewd investments than he ever did by being a rancher. He just likes to brag about owning that huge amount of land."

"Speaking of Les," said Fen. "What's your read on him?"

"He's good to Ren."

Fen heard a touch of hesitation in her voice, so he challenged her with a one-word question. "But...?"

"I've audited too many preachers' tax returns to give you an unbiased response." She seemed to search for the right words. "I have nothing but a gut instinct to go on, but I think Les would welcome a nice inheritance even more than I would. Of course, he might give it all to his church, but that would be his call."

Fen then asked, "Will Ren go home with you tonight?"

June rose from her seat. "I'll take her off your hands for two nights to give you a break."

He nodded his approval but added a condition. "As long as we get her back."

"I'm sure I won't be able to keep her away from Bailey for long."

Fen looked up in time to see Bart Hill rise from a booth and walk toward the exit. Sunny stayed long enough for Bart to make it through the door before she rose.

Lou walked toward him with an impish smile. He concluded she'd overheard Sunny and Bart's conversation.

Chapter Twenty-One

Fen held up a hand to blunt what Lou had to say. "Don't tell me what Bart and Sunny were talking about until later. I have something for you to do tonight."

A tilted head and raised eyebrows showed her suspicion. "Something tells me I won't like what you have to say."

He walked toward the door at a quick pace and lowered the volume of his words. "Do you have the home addresses for Sunny and Bart?"

"She has a condo overlooking the San Gabriel, and he lives west of town in a custom home with a pool and a three-car garage. The talk around the courthouse is that Bart does a lot of entertaining and his home is quite the showcase."

Instead of following the hallways back to the emergency room, Fen headed to the hospital's main entrance with Lou beside him. "I need confirmation that Sunny and Bart are much more than business associates. Does her condo complex have garages?"

"No garages. Covered and uncovered parking only."

"That should narrow it down to Bart's house. Get there as

quick as you can and park down the street. Unless I'm mistaken, she has an opener that operates one of Bart's three garage doors."

"How long do you want me to stay?"

He spoke in a matter-of-fact tone. "Until you're convinced she's staying the night." He paused. "One more thing: you'll need to be back on stakeout an hour before dawn. Take photos if you can."

Lou pulled up short. "What if she goes to her condo, and he goes home alone?"

"Then I'll be wrong about them."

"And I'll lose a night's sleep." Her head jerked hard to the right and left. "I'm going to swing by her condo and see if her car's there before I spend the night staring out the windshield. You're not the only one who's had a long day."

Fen didn't like her response to his plan but said nothing. Lou could be stubborn as a new mule if she thought he was sending her on a fool's errand. Then he remembered Lou was worried sick about her niece, which was probably taking its toll on her. He'd have to do a work-around.

Lou set her jaw and walked out of the hospital. Fen only made it to the door before his phone signaled an incoming text. Bailey's face and name appeared on the screen.

*Ren left with her mom. I'm bummed out and going
to bed.*

Fen's truck seemed to call his name. He was physically tired and mentally exhausted. Even so, there might be something else he could learn if he stayed around the hospital a little longer. He thought of the three brothers and realized he'd not seen Chance yet. Strange. You'd think the next in line to inherit a fortune would be the first to arrive. Perhaps he was in the waiting room.

Backtracking through the hospital brought Fen in front of the chapel. Les might have heard from Chance. The possibility was enough for him to open the door. The small room came equipped with pews, bibles, and a podium. Standing in front of the wooden lectern was a bear of a man with a full beard. He cut off his prayer at seeing the stranger standing with the door open.

"Come in, brother. We'll be glad to pray with you, for you, or for anyone else that needs it."

"Thanks. I was looking for Les Duvant." Fen's gaze passed over the men and women without success. Les wasn't there.

"Brother Les left with his brother, Chance. He should be back directly if you'd like to join us."

"Can I get a rain check on that invitation?"

"We'll be here another hour, but you can call on the Lord any time. It's a direct line that stays in service twenty-four hours a day."

Something about the man and his words hit a chord with Fen. While Sally was alive, they were regular church-goers and it wasn't out of obligation. He thought his faith was strong until her body rejected the heart that came from a young mother who'd died in a car crash. He never outright blamed God for her death, but neither had he come to terms with Him not saving her.

His father-in-law fixed the blame for Sally's death squarely on Fen because he didn't pressure her to seek another heart. Mr. Newman was the richest man in the county and wielded plenty of influence, including in the church. Fen found himself no longer welcome at his church by the paid staff. The pastor informed him it would be best for church unity if he attended a church in another town.

Fen came back to the present and realized he needed to respond to the preacher's invitation. He blurted out, "Don't wait for me, but I'd like to speak to you sometime."

Fen didn't know why he'd spoken this to the stranger, but it burst forth like water under high pressure. He was on automatic pilot as he wandered his way back to the waiting room. He stepped out of the mental fog and into a room filled with anxious and bored faces. Neither Chance nor Les were there.

The doors swished shut behind him as he looked up and down the sidewalk. Voices in the distance cut through the night air like a sharp knife. He set off to the grove of trees where he and Les had spoken earlier. The closer he got, the louder and harsher the words sounded. He arrived in time to see Les squeeze his fists into clubs and deliver a right cross that would make a boxing coach proud. Chance crumpled to the ground in a pile of blue denim. Les took flight, not checking to see if his brother would get up or not.

Fen arrived as Chance came to his senses. His left hand cupped his chin as he sat on his backside with boots stuck straight out. Moans accompanied the shaking of his head.

"Are you all right?" asked Fen.

"Huh?" asked Chance as he shook his head again and focused. "Oh. It's you. I'll be all right when the trees and moon stop swaying."

"Do you want to go inside and have a doc check you out? That was quite a punch you took."

"No doctors. I'll be back in the saddle tomorrow."

"You never saw the punch coming, did you?" asked Fen.

Chance continued to rub his chin. "I should have known that someday he'd finally grow a backbone. It surprises me that it took Dad almost dying to do it."

Fen squatted so he wouldn't have to look down on Chance.

"You must have given him a hard time when you were growing up."

"That was the extent of Dad and Grandpa's parenting skills. They drilled it into us that life was hard, so we needed to be tougher. Disputes were best settled with fists." He seemed to look into the past and then refocused. "Let me correct that. We had cheap kid-size boxing gloves. They had enough padding in them to keep us from cutting each other's face. That would have meant a trip to get sewn up and would have interfered with work."

"What caused today's altercation?"

"I pushed him until he snapped," said Chance without a hint of remorse. "I did it to see if all that Bible-thumping is real or not. Deep down, he's still the ornery little cuss he was as a kid. He still hates Dad for the things we had to do when we were growing up."

"It sounds like there's anger in both of you."

"I work mine out on the ranch. Sweat therapy is what I call it. Les tries to pray his out. Doesn't look to me like it's working too well for him."

"Oh, I don't know," said Fen. "He's still standing and you're the one sitting on his rump."

"You got me on that one. I thought he'd gone soft, but he sure put me down." Chance looked in the direction Les had taken. "Next time I'll suggest we put on boxing gloves before I accuse him of trying to kill Dad."

"Do you believe he did?"

"I doubt it, but I stopped at the wreck and spoke with Sheriff Rhoads on my way here. He let me see the bullet hole in Dad's truck. It might not be Les, but somebody tried to kill Dad."

Fen stood, spread his legs to brace himself, and extended

his hand. "Let's get you upright and make sure the trees aren't moving."

The man only swayed once before he found his footing.

There was one more question Fen needed to ask. "Did Stony ask you where you were when someone took a shot at your father?"

"He slipped it into the conversation. I was pulling a dead calf out of a heifer. Lost both of them."

"That's tough," said Fen without emotion. It was the way one cattleman would commiserate with another.

Chance gave the expected response. "Grandpa and Dad were right. Life on a ranch isn't for the weak."

Fen considered going back to the chapel but decided against it. He'd had his full measure of the Duvant family for one day. There was one more chore to take care of early the next morning, but nothing else on his calendar. What he needed more than anything was a decent night's sleep and a full day of painting. That was his plan, but murder investigations have a nasty habit of throwing a wrench into even the best-laid plans.

Chapter Twenty-Two

The alarm on Fen's phone brought him out of a dreamless sleep at four-thirty the next morning. He'd turned the volume down so as not to rouse Bailey or Lou. He then slipped into the clothes he'd worn the day before. With boots in hand, he tiptoed down the hall, into the living room, and out the front door. Once on the porch, he pulled on his boots and moved toward his truck, which he'd parked on the street. The clatter of the diesel engine was enough to rouse a light sleeper, but he knew neither Lou nor Bailey qualified. He calculated he had at least an hour and a half to complete his missions and return before they realized he'd left without telling them his plan.

With his first task completed, he still had half an hour to make a quick trip to a pastry shop and surprise them with something decadent to go along with the cooked sausage Thelma had left them.

His early morning plan worked to perfection. He was drinking coffee in a recliner when Lou made a not-so-grand appearance, wearing a tattered robe that hid whatever sleepwear she might have had on. She walked through the living room without a word. The clink of a porcelain cup on the marble countertop confirmed his suspicion that she'd soon join him with her own stimulant.

Neither spoke until Lou lowered her mug to the coffee table after nursing it for at least four minutes. "Did you go out this morning?"

He didn't want to give her the full story but also didn't want to start off his day with a lie. "You saw her arrive and I watched her leave." That's all that needed to be said about Sunny and Bart, so he changed the conversation. "There's a bag of assorted pastries on the counter. Help yourself."

This seemed to satisfy her. "I thought you'd go back to bed after the day you had."

"I could say the same about you. How long did you work on notes last night?"

"I cut the light out about one this morning."

Fen cast his gaze toward her. "There's something I didn't tell you that happened at the hospital."

Lou had her coffee mug halfway to her lips. As expected, her lethargy evaporated. It amazed him how quickly she could come on point when there was the smell of a story in the air. "Do I need to take notes?"

"It wouldn't hurt."

Lou's house shoes scuffed across the hardwood floor as she regained her seat with notepad and pen in hand. "I hope this is more interesting than trying to find phantom marriage licenses and divorce decrees."

"You be the judge," said Fen. "Shortly after you left, I happened upon Chance and Les Duvant. It was a one-punch knockout."

"What did Les do to deserve it?"

Fen shook his head. "You have it backward. Les took his older brother out with a single punch."

Lou's eyes opened wider and shifted from side to side. "I thought he was all about turning the other cheek."

"Apparently he ran out of cheeks."

"Details. Give me the complete story, blow by blow."

"There was only one blow." Fen described the incident with as much detail as he could recall.

Lou puffed out her cheeks. "It seems we have two brothers who learned to settle their problems with violence. Do you think it's possible either of them killed their grandfather and tried to kill their father?"

"I think it's more likely they'd kill each other by getting carried away in an argument."

"But you're not ruling them out?"

"Everyone's still a suspect."

The ringing of Fen's phone surprised him. Chuck, his attorney back in Newman County, was up early. Not a good sign.

"You don't get up this early," said Fen as a greeting.

"I do when I get a phone call from an irate sheriff. What does Lou think she's doing by writing a story like she did?"

"What story?"

"The one that appeared in the AUSTIN AMERICAN STATESMAN this morning. Sheriff Rhoads is ready to hang you two by your thumbs. You're both to be in his office by nine o'clock."

"I'll look into it and call you back," said Fen. "Tell Candy I said hello." He hung up.

Fen rose and walked to the front door.

"Who was that, and what story?"

Instead of answering, Fen went out the door without a word. He drove to the nearest convenience store and returned to the rental with a newspaper clutched in his hand.

The only evidence that Lou had moved from the spot he'd

left her in was that steam rose from a second cup of coffee. Exasperation tinged her words. "Are you ready to tell me what's wrong? What did Chuck say?"

He handed her the newspaper. The headline read MURDER AND COVER-UP IN WILLIAMSON COUNTY. A zoomed-in photo of a bullet hole in the roof support beam of Gil's truck accompanied the story.

Fen waited until Lou had read the entire story. Disbelief morphed into confusion. "Am I being accused of providing the details in this story?"

Another nod.

Lou's eyes narrowed. "Do you think I had anything to do with this?"

Fen didn't respond with gestures—only words. "I know you didn't. You weren't at the crash site. That photo had to come from someone else."

Lou was on her feet. "Of all the low-down tricks. Not only do I miss out on writing a story with legs, I get blamed for it." She paced. "Who did this?"

Fen raised his shoulders and let them drop. "Whoever it was wants us back in Newman County."

Lou took a stab at accusing someone. "I bet it was that detective you told me about last night. You embarrassed him in front of the sheriff, then he got a tongue-lashing, if not suspended."

"It's possible he's the one," said Fen. "It's also possible it was any of the first responders with a cell phone or someone on the forensics crew. There's also Chance Duvant. The sheriff allowed him onto the crime scene."

Lou stopped pacing. "What are you going to do about this?"

"I have a nine o'clock appointment with Stony."

"I'm going with you."

Fen shook his head. "Not this time."

"Why not? I'm the one they're accusing of dishing dirt."

"You're too valuable. If you go, your mouth will overload your common sense and you'll wind up in jail."

"It won't be the first time."

"I'm well aware of that, and it's the reason you're staying here with Bailey. You'll write a dynamite story about this development and Bailey will paint. I'll be back after I peel Stony off the ceiling and we'll all practice our crafts."

"I hate not being able to defend myself," said Lou in a sulking voice.

"Take solace in knowing you'll have the last laugh." He quirked a smile. "The pastries should help. I'll pick up some more on the way home. I have a feeling we're all going to need plenty of comfort food today."

"Chocolate," said Lou with emphasis. "The more, the better."

Bailey picked that moment to enter and fall into a chair. "What's this about pastries and chocolate?"

Fen announced, "Look in the kitchen when you're ready for breakfast. The donuts were still warm when I picked them up this morning. I hope a dozen is enough for you."

"Yum. Brain food for a starving artist."

Fen fried three eggs to accompany two sausage patties and a cinnamon roll. The two women abstained from anything high in protein, going for a sugar rush instead. His next step was to push the living room furniture against the walls. He then went to his truck and retrieved a drop cloth and everything he needed to work on his painting of the San Gabriel River after he returned from his appointment with the sheriff.

It came as no surprise when Fen received instructions from an unsmiling deputy to have a seat in an interview room until Sheriff Rhoads was ready to see him. Fen knew it was part of the game people in authority play when they want to express their displeasure. He also knew the best defense was sometimes a strong offense.

Fen looked at his watch. "Tell Stony I'm leaving in ten minutes. He knows where to find me after that."

"I wouldn't leave if I were you," said the deputy.

"You're not me." Fen gave him a toothy grin. "Run along and tell him what I said."

Nine minutes later, the deputy led Fen through locked doors and down a hallway. He gave three sharp knocks on the sheriff's door.

"Enter," came the command that reminded Fen of a Doberman's bark.

"Good morning," said Fen in a chipper tone.

Stony looked past him. "Where's that troublemaker newspaper reporter? I told your lawyer I wanted both of you here this morning."

"I told Lou she didn't need to come."

A cold glare came from the man behind the desk.

Fen threw a fresh newspaper on the sheriff's desk. "I'm doing you a favor by not bringing Lou here. She'd chew you up and spit out the pieces of your backside if you accused her of involvement in this story. She's not the source."

"What are you talking about? You discovered the bullet hole in Gil's truck and took pictures of it with your phone. I saw you." He banged a stubby finger on the newspaper and stared at him. "You and that reporter got together and sold the story to Austin's top newspaper. There are too many details in this article for it not to come from you two."

"Look closer to home," countered Fen as he pointed to the newspaper. He then handed his phone to Stony. "Here are all the photos I took. The one in the paper isn't among them. Lou has seen none of my photos yet. We were at the hospital trying to find out who killed Gilbert and almost killed Gil."

Fen remained quiet as Stony made sure the photos didn't match. He wasn't over being mad but the deep sigh showed that his emotional tide had turned. "All I know is there's a murder, an attempted murder, and my department is catching grief from all sides. I don't like it, and I'm going to do something about it."

Chapter Twenty-Three

F en settled into a chair, wondering what the sheriff would do about the disparaging newspaper story. "I don't blame you, but things like that happen when bodies show up where they're not supposed to be. If it's any consolation, I think we made progress at the hospital last night. If I'm not mistaken, Gilbert's killer came to check on Gil."

"I hope you have a name."

"Not yet, but I'm close to eliminating several suspects."

Stony shook his head. "I sent detectives there, but you'd already talked to everyone of interest. Should have known you'd seize the opportunity."

"Do you have time for me to give you a report on who we spoke with and what they said?"

"I'd appreciate it. It will also give me an idea of how much information my detectives missed. I can't fire them all, but I have a feeling there's one or two who'll go back on patrol before this case is over."

"Cases," said Fen, correcting the sheriff. "There's two after yesterday."

It took a while for Fen to relay what had transpired at the hospital. The biggest reaction came when he told the tale of Les slugging Chance.

"I wish I'd been there to see that," said Stony. "It's hard for me to imagine Les blowing his top and putting Chance on his back. Makes me wonder what else the middle brother is capable of."

"Or why Chance pushed him to the breaking point," countered Fen. "I guess there's a little Cain and Abel in all brothers."

Stony interlaced his fingers behind his head and summarized. "It seems all the suspects are family."

"Not all, but most. I still don't have a handle on Robert, the youngest brother. His wife was nothing like I expected. An auditor for the IRS and a nightclub musician are a strange mix. It's hard for me to imagine two people who are that different not having tension in their marriage. June told me she wouldn't mind if she and Robert received a fat inheritance."

Stony gave a nod. "Are you planning on interviewing him today?"

"It's my day for deep thinking. That means I'll spend all day painting."

"What about tomorrow?"

"I'm supposed to meet with Les at a coffee shop early in the morning. I need to confirm the appointment with him after what I witnessed last night."

An idea sprang into Fen's mind. "Why don't you give your detectives a chance to redeem themselves? Send them to Austin to interview Robert. We need to verify where he was when someone took a shot at Gil. Also, if they could bring Ren back to where we're staying, it would save her parents a trip."

"Consider it done," said Stony. "She's such a likable little magpie. It will do those detectives good to be around someone with a positive attitude."

Stony leaned forward. "You said I should look closer to home if I wanted to find out who gave this photo and inside information to the press." He held up the newspaper. "How close?"

Fen had asked himself the same question but hadn't come up with a definite answer. "Whoever it is wants me and my crew out of town. They counted on getting a knee-jerk reaction out of you. That tells me they know you pretty well."

Stony's gaze drifted to the door behind Fen. He refocused and tapped the newspaper again. "They had to be at the crash site last night in order to take this photo."

Fen nodded in partial agreement. "It could also mean they want credit for discovering who killed Gilbert."

"Unless my detectives wake up and do their job, you'll deserve all the credit."

Fen countered with, "We may be ahead on interviews, but we still need a big break."

A question came to Fen. "Has the forensic report come back yet on the identity of the body Ren and Bailey found?"

"It came in late yesterday afternoon. No surprises. It's Gibert Duvant. As soon as you leave, my department spokesperson will occupy the chair you're in and we'll hammer out a press release." Stony reared back in his chair. "If someone in this department gave the photo and story to the press, they'll think an anvil fell on them by the time I get through." He righted himself. "I have an idea, but you might not like it."

"Won't know until I hear it."

"Let's cause a scene when you leave."

The corners of Fen's mouth pulled up. "Do you want them to think you're furious with me and it was my plan to embarrass your detectives?"

"Exactly. I'll be looking for the rooster who crows the loudest and struts more than the rest."

Fen scratched his chin. "That might work. I'll let you know if anyone contacts me who seems too proud of themselves." Fen gazed into a corner of the ceiling. "You know, this could help motivate your people to work harder on the cases. Some of them resent me for being here."

"I resented you," said Stony. He stood. "Don't hold back on giving back to me what I'm about to give you. Of course, it's all a show."

Fen chuckled. "This could be a cathartic therapy session for both of us."

The back-and-forth hollering started as soon as Fen opened the sheriff's door and didn't stop until the front door to the building closed behind him. Accusations of incompetence flew like confetti in front of a fan. The word would soon be out that Fen and Lou brought disgrace upon the sheriff's department and the sheriff had read him the riot act.

On his way to the truck, Fen thought about the mistakes the sheriff's detectives had made. Perhaps the killer had made mistakes, too. It was also possible he, Lou, and Bailey hadn't recognized something already revealed.

It was time to paint and think and plan their next steps. In some ways, investigating was like deer hunting. Instead of spending time and energy stalking a buck, all a person has to do is climb into an elevated stand and wait for the deer to come to them.

On the other hand, sometimes you could spend an entire hunting season in a stand waiting and never put meat on the table. Only one way to find out... go back to the rental and lose himself in painting the San Gabriel River.

Lou met him at the front door when he pushed it open. "Can you do without me for a day or two?"

"Is something wrong?"

"My editor called. There's a scandal brewing in Newman County. He wants me to get ahead of it."

Fen asked, "Money or something else?"

"Money for sure, but I'm going to find out if there's another angle to the story. There's money missing from Gwen Lewis' escrow account."

"The attorney?"

Lou gave her head a firm nod.

"How long since she moved from Austin?"

"Five years."

"Speaking of attorneys," said Fen. "Did you check with Chuck about common-law marriages?"

"Chuck gave me a word-salad of legal terms and court cases. I told him to put Candy on the line and she simplified it for me. It's actually pretty cut and dried. If there's a license or the two parties register the relationship as a common-law marriage, they're married. Anything less than that can mean a trial if either party objects. My research showed there's nothing on file at the courthouse between Gil and Prissy."

Fen interrupted. "Something tells me you're going to say, 'But...'"

"You're right. Candy said without certificates of marriage or divorce, the decision can go either way. She described it as whoever has the most physical evidence that showed them to be married, which side did the best job of selecting a sympathetic jury, and who has the best attorney."

It was the answer Fen expected, so he shifted back to Lou's original question about her going home to cover the story. "Do you think two days will be enough to get the story?"

"It should be unless the people who lost money don't talk."

"Do you know who they are?"

"My editor gave me two names."

"Call Thelma on your way home. She'll know every fact and rumor." He took a breath. "Be sure to tell her how much we're enjoying the food she left us."

"I won't have to stretch the truth for that."

"I agree," said Bailey as she looked up from her painting.

Lou retreated to her bedroom and came out with an overnight bag. She gave a quick wave goodbye. "I'll be back. Don't you dare solve the case until I return." She paused. "By the way, how did it go with the sheriff?"

"He threw me out of his office."

Bailey came alive. "You're joking."

He chuckled. "Sort of. He's intent on finding out who tipped off the press. He came up with a plan that paints me and you as the bad guys."

Lou dropped her bag and tented her hands on her hips. "That means nobody will talk to me when I return."

Fen shifted his gaze to Lou. "By the way, the forensic report came back, and the sheriff gave me a copy. It's not only an official homicide, but there's some interesting details."

"I want a copy."

Fen shook his head. "Not until you return."

"What?"

He couldn't help but laugh at her reaction. "I want to make sure you'll come back. Besides, you have a scandal to keep you busy for the next couple of days."

Lou glared at him. "Men like you give me gray hair."

The door clicked shut instead of slamming, which told him Lou wasn't as upset as she pretended to be.

"You like pulling Lou's chain," said Bailey.

Fen countered with, "We all need to focus on something besides the cases. Painting for you and me, and a scandal back home for Lou."

The day passed without many words. Neither artist broke

for lunch. He was teaching Bailey to follow his example of reaching flow as soon as possible and staying in that mental state as long as she could. She was an excellent pupil and could last almost as long as he could.

It was late afternoon when a knock sounded on the door and broke their concentration. Fen stuck his brush in solvent and put his palate on a vintage folding TV tray. He then strode to the door and opened it.

"Hello, Bart. Come in and meet my protégé, Bailey Madison."

Chapter Twenty-Four

Bart Hill accepted Fen's offer for a cup of coffee, but not before he stopped at Fen's unfinished painting of the San Gabriel. Admiration gushed. "Even though this is unfinished, I can tell it will be something special." He peeled his gaze from the canvas. "It's pure genius to put a Model A Ford on the bridge as it must have looked back then."

"It's a long way from being finished," said Fen.

Bart shifted to examine Bailey's work. "I can see Fen's influence on you, but there's something a bit more daring in your brush strokes."

"It's called inexperience," said Bailey in a matter-of-fact tone.

"I think not," said Bart as he cupped his chin in his hand. "I'd call it refreshingly unique. You have your own style that pays homage to your mentor without compromising who you are."

"If you mean I'm impetuous and too opinionated, you're right."

Bart kept his chin in his hand and moved closer to her work. "You're bold. I can't wait to see this in my gallery."

Fen noticed Bart's nails had received a recent manicure. He gave the man a haircut-to-shoes once-over. He looked like a Ken doll come to life.

"About that coffee," said Fen. "Have a seat at the table." He looked at Bailey. "Let's spoil our supper and have a piece of Thelma's German chocolate cake with our coffee."

"That won't spoil my supper. I'm starving."

Small talk about painting filled the time while coffee brewed and Bailey served slices of cake on paper plates. Fen had to admit that Bart had no trouble filling the time with banter. He raved about the quality of the cake after taking the first bite.

Halfway through his cake, Bart allowed his fork to rest on the plate. "The reason I stopped by was to firm up your commitment to do a showing of your work in my gallery."

"I thought that's why you came," said Fen. "I like the idea, but most of my works these days are commissions. I'd be lucky to fill one wall of your gallery."

"Oh," said Bart with disappointment creasing his brow.

"However," said Fen. "I think I know how this could work."

"I'd love to hear it."

"The exhibition needs a theme. I'll have my painting of the San Gabriel and may have time to knock out a few more. The same for Bailey. Use paintings of the river as the theme and invite local artists to take part."

Bart sat up straight. "Genius. Pure genius." He shifted his gaze to Bailey. "I insist we include your work."

"You won't get a complaint from me. I've never had my work shown in a gallery."

"Then it's settled. What do you two think about a show this summer?"

Both Fen and Bailey nodded their approval. Bailey added, "That will give Ren time to paint something."

"Ren Duvant?" asked Bart. "I thought her medium was large-scale murals on buildings."

"Primarily, that's true," said Fen. "But she's a diamond in the rough. I've challenged her to broaden her horizons by painting something on the scale of what Bailey and I are working on. Her sketches show great potential."

"That's good enough for me," said Bart with excitement in his voice. "This kind of thinking is what's going to transform this old town into a modern city." He changed his last statement. "Of course, it's nostalgia that sells, too."

Fen put out a piece of verbal bait to see how he'd react. "I've found that safe cities attract growth."

Bart all but pounced on the words. "You're absolutely right. That article in today's Austin newspaper was so unfortunate. It showed the sheriff's department to be a bunch of rubes. That they declared a murder an accident isn't the publicity we want."

He shifted his gaze to Bailey. "Is it true that you and Ren discovered the body?"

"It was weird and awful at the same time. All we could see was a hand and a bit of the arm, but that was more than enough."

The ringing of Bailey's phone prompted her to excuse herself and walk into the living room. Muffled words drifted into the kitchen. They were too soft to make out what Bailey was saying.

Bart shifted his gaze to Fen. "The rumor going around is that you're helping the sheriff uncover the truth about Gilbert Duvant's death."

"I was," said Fen. "The sheriff let me know this morning that his department didn't need my help."

"Had you made any progress in your investigation?"

"Not enough. It's a tough case to crack. It wouldn't surprise me if it goes unsolved."

"I heard another rumor you went to the crash site and discovered someone shot Gil's truck."

"First responders would have found it. I got lucky and guessed right."

"You're too modest. You have a reputation of regularly guessing right."

Bailey returned with an announcement for Fen. "That was Ren. Prissy wants you to call her. Something about doing a pencil sketch of her dog, Adonis."

Fen nodded. "I owe her one. I'll call her tonight." He used the opportunity to get the conversation off of himself and onto Bart. "Have you ever had any dealings with Prissy Duvant?"

"I pawned her off on an assistant a long time ago. She's obsessed with opening a pet cemetery. It's an untested idea in this county, has limited support, and not enough financial backing."

Bart produced what looked like a well-practiced salesman's smile. "It's a shame anyone would chase after such a scheme when this county is exploding with genuine opportunities. I don't have fingers and toes enough to count the ways a forward-thinking person could have money chasing them down the street."

Fen smiled back but didn't respond. He wanted to see how long Bart would dangle bait in front of him.

"Yes, sir," said Bart. "This is one of the fastest-growing counties in the nation and people with vision will reap the rewards for the rest of their lives and those of their heirs."

"I don't have any children." He said this to see if it would slow down the sales pitch. It didn't.

"You're a handsome man with many good years ahead of

you. Even if you don't remarry, you'll continue to accumulate. You're a man who doesn't have to paint, but you do, and your works command handsome prices. Think of all the good you could do both during your life and after you're gone if you doubled your wealth."

Fen had heard enough. "You're right about my desire to paint. I also enjoy working with my farm and ranch manager when he needs help. Of course, the oil checks make work optional. Between those vocations, I have more than enough to keep me busy." He took a breath and gave his own toothy smile. "When that isn't enough, my phone will ring and someone will ask me to help solve a murder."

Bart kept smiling. "I can honestly say I've never met a true Renaissance man until today. I congratulate you on being a success in everything you put your hand to."

"Not everything," said Fen. "I failed in finding the person who killed Gilbert Duvant."

"That's because our narrow-minded sheriff won't let you finish what you started."

"Do you think I should keep investigating even though the sheriff told me not to?"

"I do," said Bailey. "Who gives a rip what the sheriff says?"

Bart lost his smile. "I'm not sure that's such a good idea. This is a real law-and-punishment county. The sheriff and his minions may have cut corners with the original investigation, but today's newspaper article will motivate them to redouble their efforts."

Fen turned to Bailey. "Listen to Mr. Hill. He has his pulse on what goes on in this county. Sometimes, all it takes is someone to come in and stir the pot. We've done that and now it's up to the sheriff's detectives to find the killer."

Bailey played along. "I guess you're right. How long will we stay here without a case to work on?"

"It depends on how many paintings we want to complete for the show at Mr. Hill's gallery."

Fen turned to Bart. "You know every inch of the county. Where would you suggest we go to paint?"

Bart pushed his lips together as he considered the question. "There's Lake Georgetown, which was formed when they built a dam on the north branch of the San Gabriel. Blue Hole, which is in town and a favorite place to swim. You can't beat San Gabriel Park and the old concrete bridge."

"Great suggestions," said Fen. "I went to the park. The sheer rock walls on the south side of the river almost begged me to paint them. The ducks and squirrels added a pleasant touch."

Bart rose from his chair. "I'm so excited about working with both of you and putting on the best gallery show this county has ever seen. Leave all the details to me."

Fen rose and extended a hand. Bailey, however, simply gave a weak attempt at smiling.

After walking Bart to the door, Bailey came into the living room. "I don't like him," she said with sandpaper in her words. "Do we have to do a show in his gallery?"

"It may not come to that."

"Do you think he killed Ren's great-grandfather?"

"He's too cunning to do it himself."

"That tells me you think he's somehow involved."

"I didn't say that. We need to plan a trip to the three places he told us about. I believed him when he said those are excellent locations."

Bailey ran her tongue over her front teeth. "He's a slimeball."

"That doesn't make him a killer."

"No, but it makes me want to brush and floss."

"Good idea. After we get rid of the foul taste, we'll go find Blue Hole."

Bailey walked toward the hall. "I can use some fresh air after Bart Hill."

Blue Hole proved to be close to their rental, on a street that stopped at the south branch of the San Gabriel. The trip refreshed both of them and they returned home with sketches, photos, and better attitudes.

What Fen wasn't expecting was a pickup truck to pull up behind them.

Chapter Twenty-Five

Fen tried to identify the man as he exited the truck and closed the door behind him. "Cory? Is that you?"

"It's me," said the young man dressed in jeans, a pullover shirt, and tennis shoes.

"I didn't recognize you without your uniform and patrol truck. Come in and get something to drink."

"Thanks," said the deputy. "Don't mind if I do."

Bailey joined the conversation. "Hey, Cory. If you came to see Ren, you're out of luck. Her mom took her to Austin last night."

Cory waved away the comment. "I heard. Her mom's always been protective of her. If it weren't for her dad, Ren would be stuck in a nine-to-five job in Austin."

Fen walked ahead and unlocked the door as Cory and Bailey took their time walking up the sidewalk. This gave him a few seconds to wonder why Deputy Cory came to see them when he knew Ren was in Austin.

Once inside, Fen asked, "Coffee, tea, or water? That's all we have."

"I'll have whatever you're having," said Cory.

Fen looked closer at Cory's features. His dual training as a state trooper and an artist made the inspection second nature to him. Details were essential for both professions. His mind rolled off a physical description that read like a radio broadcast of a suspect. *Subject is a white male, early twenties, five-ten, one-eighty, short dark hair, clean shaven, no visible scars or tattoos.*

Bailey said, "I'm having decaf coffee."

"Make it two," said Cory.

"Three," said Fen.

Bailey busied herself in the kitchen while Fen and Cory took seats at the table. Fen eased into the conversation. "Is this your day off?"

"Today and tomorrow. I need to get some overtime off the books. The wreck last night put me way over."

Fen gave a nod and remembered what his job as sheriff was like. "Getting employees' time off the books drove me nuts. Some deputies burned it off with no problem, while others hoarded it like gold. Then, they'd want to string together a bunch of days to go along with a holiday or their scheduled days off."

"My sergeant doesn't give me an option. I can be two hours into a shift and he'll tell me to go home."

"That's one way," said Fen. "It doesn't do much for morale, but it keeps the higher-ups off his back." He chuckled. "You're reminding me of why I'm glad I don't have to deal with scheduling shifts anymore. Those and budgets are enough to make a preacher cuss."

Bailey delivered a steaming mug to Cory. "I hope you two don't mind me serving last night's leftovers reheated in the microwave. It seemed a shame to throw out so much."

"No problem," said Cory. "You wouldn't believe how bad

some of the coffee is in convenience stores between midnight and five in the morning."

"Amen to that," said Fen. He then allowed silence to settle in without trying to force the conversation. Cory knew Ren was in Austin, so he had some other reason to stop by.

Silence was on the verge of becoming uncomfortable when Bailey delivered Fen's coffee and slipped into a chair.

"You're not having any?" asked Cory.

"I decided I better not. I need a steady hand, and it makes me jittery."

"Even if it's decaf?" asked Cory.

Bailey shrugged. "It's probably all in my head, but one or two cups in the morning is my quota until a cup of decaf when I've finished painting for the day."

Fen didn't want to sit waiting for Cory to tell him the reason for his visit. He thought he knew but needed to verify it. He turned to look at the young man. "How long did you have to direct traffic last night?"

"Until the wee hours of the morning. I thought it wouldn't take that long, but then I waved the forensics crew through. That told me the wreck wasn't a normal accident." He looked at Fen. "Is it true that you discovered the bullet hole?"

Fen nodded.

"How did you know to look for it?"

"I'd seen something similar before."

"A deputy told me the sheriff blew his stack and sent the lead detective home. I think he was angry because of the murder case."

"Wouldn't you be mad if you were sheriff?"

"I guess so."

"I left before the forensics crew arrived. What all did they do?"

Excitement filled Cory's words. "All sorts of things. I

traded places with a fellow deputy, so I had a front-row view. They measured skid marks, set up a gizmo that pinpointed the trajectory of the shot, went over the truck from top to bottom to check for any additional bullet holes, did a grid search of the area, did a full inventory of everything in the truck, and took at least a hundred photos. The only thing I got to help with was the search."

Fen asked, "Did they locate the round that was fired?"

Cory's head seemed to bounce like a plastic dog's head on a dashboard. "Not that hard to find with a metal detector after they had the trajectory."

Fen concluded that Cory had no trouble talking once he got going. It was time to give the young man a test of sorts. "There's something that has me scratching my head. What does the murder of Gilbert Duvant have to do with someone trying to kill his son?"

Cory puffed out his cheeks. "I was going to ask you that very question. Any ideas?"

Fen chuckled. "Ideas are simple to come by. There's no shortage of suspects, so I can come up with a scenario for six or eight people with no problem."

"Like who?"

Fen leaned forward. "There's a young man who knows that area of the county and the people who live there like they were family. He also knows the habits of everyone involved and keeps a close eye on the Duvant ranch. He even came to the fire that was supposed to have killed old man Gilbert." Fen tilted his head. "Do you believe in coincidences?"

"Not as a rule."

"Then try this on. What are the chances that this same person was at last night's crash site?"

"Really? Who is he?"

Bailey let out a low moan. "You, goober. Fen's pulling your leg. Can't you see he's talking about you?"

A quick intake of air accompanied a look of abject fear.

Fen slapped his hand on the table and let out a roar of laughter.

Bailey shook her head as she looked at Cory. "Don't feel too bad. He pulls things like that on me from time to time. It's a major character defect."

The pink hues on Cory's face receded by the time Fen stopped laughing. He finally said, "Now you can see how easy it is to come up with suspects. You need to ask who had motive, means, and opportunity and let hard evidence eliminate suspects."

Cory looked down into his cup of coffee. "The rumor going around is the sheriff threw you out of his office today."

"No rumor," said Fen. "It's a fact."

"So you're not trying to solve the case?"

"I work with the authorities by invitation. You can see by the easels in the living room that Bailey and I are spending our day painting. Lou, my research assistant, is already back in Newman County."

Fen shot Bailey a look that he hoped would communicate that she didn't need to add anything to what he'd said.

Cory pushed the remnants of his coffee away. "I hate to say this, but I'm not sure our detectives have what it takes to solve the murder, or last night's shooting."

A sly smile pulled on the left corner of Fen's mouth. "I can tell you from way too much experience that most crimes aren't solved."

Bailey quickly added, "He's talking about me. I might have gotten by with a few things when I was younger in Houston." She winked. "I'm now a mostly reformed woman."

Cory pointed an index finger at her. "Now you're trying to jerk my chain like Sheriff Maguire did."

"Speaking of dog chains," said Fen as he looked at Cory. "What do you make of Billy not being in the grave with Gilbert?"

"That tells me Billy was in the fire. One mystery solved."

"What if he wasn't in the fire?"

Cory stood. "Are you saying he wasn't?"

"Not at all. That explanation makes the most sense, but I like to keep my mind open to other possibilities."

"Thanks for the coffee and the conversation. Talking to someone with so much experience makes me realize how much I have to learn."

Bailey saw Cory to the door and soon returned while Fen rinsed the cups. "Why do you think he really stopped by?"

Fen looked out the window over the sink into the backyard. "A better question to ask is who sent him?"

Bailey spoke with certainty. "I think it's the detectives. They want to make sure we're not still working on the case."

"Didn't you hear Cory say the sheriff threw me out and told me he didn't want our help?"

She hooked her hair behind her ears. "There's a big difference between hearing and believing. What's our next step?"

"Painting the rest of the day, followed by a dish of lasagna Thelma left for us. Tomorrow morning, I'm meeting with Les Duvant to ask him more questions about why he slugged his brother."

"What about me?"

"Paint until Ren gets back. She's close to her Uncle Les and his family. Find out if the outbursts of anger are more common than he wants anyone to know."

Fen waited for a few ticks of the clock. "One more thing. I

think someone told Cory to come here and pump us for information. Try to find out who it was."

"I already told you. It's the detectives who messed up the original investigation."

Fen shook his head. "We're swimming in deeper waters than that."

"How am I supposed to find out something like that? I barely know him."

Another quirk of a smile. "Be creative."

Chapter Twenty-Six

Streaks of what Fen would describe as the color *blushing rose* shot forth from the east between puffy early morning clouds. Was it an omen of stormy weather or something more sinister? Time would tell. But first, he needed his morning ritual with Sally.

After a shorter than usual time with his wife, he parked on the edge of a mostly empty parking lot, breathing in the crisp air as he walked to the door of Just Love Coffee Cafe. A neon sign winked OPEN at him and a friendly voice behind a counter bid him good morning. He approached the college-age woman and ordered a medium dark roast. He'd intentionally arrived fifteen minutes early for his six-thirty appointment with Les Duvant.

Clusters of men were meeting, some with open bibles, while the more tech-savvy followed along looking down at their phones. He settled in a remote corner of the room and thought how dissimilar his meeting would be from that of the other patrons.

Fen took his first pleasant sip of the bold coffee and reconsidered his last thought. The patrons, who now included a few women, seemed to be looking for answers to life's questions. He, too, was looking for answers. Who killed Gilbert Duvant, and who tried to kill his son?

The cup was half empty when Les strode through the door. Fen rose and met him as he approached the counter. "Thanks for coming," he said. "Order whatever you want. I'm getting the Flying Pig."

"Good choice. I'll have a breakfast taco."

"Only one?"

"I'm sort of fasting so I can concentrate on prayer. I didn't eat at all yesterday and was feeling lightheaded by the end of the day."

Fen pivoted and faced the young woman waiting to take their order. "One Flying Pig, one breakfast taco for here, and one to go." He turned back to Les. "Just in case you get wobbly again."

"Thanks." He faced the woman. "I'd like a small cup of regular coffee with the taco, please."

Fen asked, "Don't you want a large or at least a medium?"

The barista spoke up. "Refills of regular coffee are free. Robert always drinks one and takes one with him."

Fen thrust his cup toward the smiling young lady. "In that case, fill it up. What a deal. You are now my favorite coffee shop in the entire state." The amount of the order showed up on a computer screen and he paid the bill.

Les said, "Go find a seat. I'll get my coffee and be right with you. They'll deliver our food when it's ready."

A gentle rumble of voices filled the coffee shop, but it was soft enough to still carry on private conversations. Fen sat with his back to a wall. He hoped this would keep distractions to a minimum for Les.

After greeting a couple of men, Les arrived at the two-person table that Fen had picked out. He placed his paper cup on the table and removed the black plastic lid. Aromatic steam rose.

Fen started the interview by asking, "How many of the people in here do you know?"

This earned a grin. "About half. A few years back it would have been more. Our town is large enough now you can't know everyone." Les's smile disappeared. "I need to ask for your forgiveness. My actions with Chance are inexcusable."

Fen leaned forward and whispered, "It wasn't me you slugged."

He nodded a partial affirmation to what Fen had said. "True, but you were there, and I need to make amends to everyone. That includes anyone who witnessed it."

"Have you talked to Chance?"

"I called him several times yesterday. He hung up on me the first time. My phone calls have gone to voicemail ever since, and he doesn't respond to my texts."

Fen took in the information. Something didn't add up. "I spoke with Chance after the incident. He said he wound you up on purpose. Do you think his actions since then could be a continuation of him playing that same game?"

"It doesn't matter. There's no excuse for me slugging him and I have to apologize. It's a biblical command."

"Did you apologize in your texts?"

"Yes, but that's not good enough."

"Have you spoken with your pastor about this?"

"Not yet."

"Why not?"

Les looked down at his bruised hand and whispered, "Shame."

Fen held up his palms. "It's none of my business, but why do you want to wallow in shame and self-pity?"

"I don't," snapped Les.

"That's not true. You've already apologized to your brother."

"It's not enough."

"All right, if you insist on experiencing even more shame, I'll go to the city police and give a statement of how you assaulted your brother. If they arrest you, will that be enough shame?"

It was shock therapy, and it worked to reveal a side of Les that Fen thought might lurk under the surface. Les's fists clenched into meaty clubs. "Don't you dare," he said in a strained voice. "I'll lose my job and my good name."

"Why not? It would help you along your path to becoming a martyr."

"The only path I want to walk on is the path of peace."

Fen pointed. "Walking through life with clenched fists is a hard thing to do. I don't think it's permitted on the path of peace."

Les relaxed his hands, but his squinted eyes betrayed the rage that boiled within.

It was time to back off and take another route to get Les to reveal information that would help solve the cases. Fen softened his words. "I'm not going to the police. What happened was a family matter. It would be none of my business if you and Chance weren't suspects in the death of your grandfather and the attempted murder of your father."

"I had nothing to do with those."

"Then why did detectives grill you for answers yesterday?"

Anger flared again. "How did you know?"

Fen shrugged. "It's what I'd do if I was still a sheriff." He took a sip of coffee. "Besides, you just confirmed it. They asked you hard questions, didn't they?"

"They were complete jerks. I've worked so hard since I left

home to establish a spotless reputation, and now everything's coming unraveled."

Fen took an educated guess and hoped he was right. "You resent having to work so hard to earn a living at a job you don't really like, while Chance gets to do what he loves."

Les seemed to speak before he thought. "I was always a disappointment to my father. His pet name for Chance was *Good Chance*. Do you know what he called me? *Not a Chance.* Try growing up with that! I'm still trying to live down his prophecy."

To take advantage of the middle brother speaking without thinking, Fen asked, "Would you have accepted an inheritance if the accident had killed your father?"

"Of course." His eyes shifted left to right and back again. "Then I'd give it away. That money is cursed."

Fen believed the first answer but not what followed. Time was ticking by and it seemed Les preferred to get into a theological circular argument about the evils of money rather than speak without thinking. Time to hit him with another hard question.

"Do you believe your father murdered your grandfather?"

"What a question," said Les as his head involuntarily jerked back. His face contorted as he gave the question his full attention. "There was a time when I thought him capable of it."

"But?" asked Fen to keep the flow coming.

"Grandpa was too close to death for Dad to do something that stupid. Dad's weakness is younger women, greed, and a broken moral compass. Otherwise, he's satisfied with being rich and bragging about having the biggest ranch in the county."

"He could be richer if he sold some of the land."

Les wagged his head in denial. "No way. He loves money, bragging about the ranch, and having a pretty young woman on his arm. The order of importance shifts from time to time, but not what's important to him."

"What about Chance? He came close to being the primary heir to the family fortune two nights ago. Do his priorities match your father's?"

"Not really. He's more one-dimensional. He wants to sell half of the land for residential or commercial purposes. It's pretty useless for growing prize cattle. But he also seems content with his life. That may change with time, but I don't think so. As for Dad's other businesses, Chance couldn't care less about them. It would be a misery for him to have to run those. He'd much rather let me and Robert split them as long as he gets all the land."

Their order arrived. The interruption put a quick end to the conversation until Les had wolfed down his breakfast taco. He looked longingly at the second one, wrapped in foil.

"Go ahead," said Fen. "You've already broken the fast. Might as well have plenty of energy for the day's work."

Les reached for the eggs, sausage, and cheese wrapped in a tortilla. "Don't mind if I do. Somehow, talking about my dysfunctional family helped."

Fen swallowed a bite of his breakfast and asked, "Will you try to call Chance again today?"

"Not until after I speak with my pastor and get his advice. To tell the truth, I'm not really mad at myself for slugging him. It felt good to see the surprise on his face." He chewed the first bite of his second taco and swallowed. "Still, it's not what the Bible teaches, so I'll seek godly counsel. I'm unsure about when would be the best way, or time, to apologize. What I've been doing hasn't worked."

Fen went down his mental checklist of questions to ask. He wanted it to be an open-ended question so he could enjoy his breakfast while it was still hot. "What was it like growing up on the ranch with Chance and Robert?"

"Chance was a bully, and Robert was off in his own world." Les put his taco down. "Dad believed I was weak and encouraged Chance to toughen me up. He was in college before I got big enough and strong enough to take him. He rarely came home and when he did, he steered clear of me."

"Do you think you got all that anger out of you the other night?"

Les's brow furrowed. "I think it did, but I can't promise it won't happen again if he pushes hard enough."

"I don't believe he wants a rematch," said Fen. "That right cross is not something he wants to experience again. Speaking of bullies... how hard did the detectives press you?"

"Hard. They told me there came a point in investigations when I'd have to prove my innocence. They said they'd detain me and get a warrant if I didn't give them permission to search my home and take all my firearms."

This didn't come as a surprise to Fen. It was an all-too-common tactic employed by police. It also showed how much pressure the detectives were under to solve the case.

Fen asked, "What firearms did they take?"

"My .243 deer rifle and a .9 mm Glock. They left my shotgun." He paused. "They were interested in an old .22 revolver I used to own. Someone stole it last year. I filed a police report, but they said the chances of recovery were slim. They searched the house extra-hard looking for it."

It occurred to Fen that he hadn't asked the sheriff about the results of the autopsy. He needed to make a phone call.

The conversation lagged until both men finished their breakfast, and Les checked his phone for messages. This was a sign to Fen that the meeting was coming to a close.

Fen asked, "Where were you on the day of the fire at your grandfather's home?"

"I took a group of kids from church to Schlitterbahn, a water park in New Braunfels. We didn't get home until after ten that night."

"And the night someone tried to kill your father?"

"At home, watching television with the wife and kids. Cory Blane called me and told me about Dad being in a wreck."

This statement reinforced that Deputy Cory Blane was in the vicinity of both the murder and the attempted murder. He'd also expressed a desire to advance as soon as possible.

"I'd best be getting to work," said Les as he rose. "Thanks for the breakfast, and good luck with the investigation." He then asked, "Are you getting any closer to solving either case?"

"I hope so," said Fen. "I believe what you told me today will help. Thanks."

Les went to the counter, retrieved his refill, greeted some more people on his way to the door, and left.

Fen determined his next step was to check in with Sheriff Rhoads. He needed to know if someone had used a firearm in Gilbert's death as well as the attempt to kill Gil. Also, had Les really turned in a police report claiming a break-in and a missing .22 pistol?

Fen's thought then went to Ren. Had she been there when detectives interviewed Robert, the youngest son of Gil? If so, would she tell Bailey what they discussed? Did Robert own firearms? Did the deputies trick him into letting them take the weapons like they had Les?

It was time to return to the rental, make some phone calls, and wait for Ren to return.

Chapter Twenty-Seven

Fen parked on the street when he returned from the coffee shop and used the cab of his truck as a temporary office to call the sheriff. The most important information he received was that a .22 round killed Gilbert Duvant. The trajectory was at an upward angle and entered from the base of the skull, near the spinal column.

Fen remarked that it sounded more like an execution than a crime of passion. The sheriff agreed. "Whoever shot him is a cold-blooded killer. It looks to me like someone hired it done. I told my detectives to expand their search to professionals."

Perhaps it was the jolt of caffeine from the second cup of coffee, but Fen's mind raced with faces and names of suspects. He'd considered the possibility of a hired killer but limited the scope of his investigation to local people with something to gain. He preferred to follow the mantra: *Follow the money.* Over the years, he added passion to his short list of motives. He then asked himself which of the current suspects were the greediest and most passionate. He heaved a sigh. Several came to mind. Perhaps painting would bring clarity to his thoughts.

It surprised him to find Bailey awake, dressed, and with a paintbrush in hand. She greeted him with a quick glance and a question. "How was the coffee?"

"Strong and very good. The food was a great change of pace. They can do more things with a waffle than I thought possible."

"Did you learn anything that will help us solve the cases?"

"Time will tell. I need to call Lou and tell her to come back as soon as she can. We need to put our heads together and compare notes."

"If you call her now, she could be back before sundown."

"There's still one brother we need to find out about, and one thing after the next has kept me from fully concentrating on painting. You know what a couple days of uninterrupted painting do for me."

"Yeah. You solve murders."

"Have you heard from Ren?"

"Not yet. She said her dad sleeps until mid-afternoon most days. I don't expect her to be back until this evening."

Fen moved to his easel and frowned at his work. It wasn't as far along as he'd hoped. Turning to face Bailey, he said, "Don't bet on Ren's dad sleeping late today. Detectives like to keep a suspect on their back foot. Rousting people out of bed is a common tactic."

"Why do they do that?"

"It doesn't give them time to make up lies."

Bailey looked at her canvas. "My brain doesn't work until I've had coffee. I can see how that would work."

"Exactly," said Fen. "Hit them early with tough questions, then listen carefully to how they respond. If they're trying to be deceptive, they'll likely forget what they said. Later, reword the questions and ask again. It's hard to remember the details of what you've already said. The detectives will then use the suspect's inconsistencies as leverage against them."

"I'd tell them to take a long walk off a short pier if cops ever woke me up in the middle of the night."

"There's a better way to handle the police."

"Like what?"

"That's a conversation for another time. Today I want you focused on your painting."

He changed the subject. "Did you eat breakfast?"

"I had half a dozen pigs-in-blankets that Thelma left. I love those little sausages wrapped in a biscuit."

"That should get you by until lunch. Let's paint."

Hours passed in silence. Bailey preferred to paint with earbuds playing something he couldn't hear. He liked a quiet room and made good progress in his rendering of the San Gabriel River. The ringing of his phone interrupted his flow at 11:45 a.m.

"Good morning, Prissy," he said after checking the caller ID. "What can I do for you?"

"I know this is a big imposition, but I was wondering if you could come by and do a sketch of Adonis? He's still jealous of you drawing Donavan and not him."

Fen rolled his eyes but agreed to take a break after lunch and go to the home of Gil Duvant's self-proclaimed ex-wife. "I haven't heard how Gil's doing today. Did you run by the hospital and check on him?"

"He's being released this afternoon. I went by to see him but didn't stay long. Sunny was there playing Florence Nightingale. She's such a lovely lady. Too bad she can't marry him."

Fen filed her statement away and set a time to be at her house. It wouldn't take long to knock out an acceptable drawing. He could be back before Ren arrived.

Bailey was wrist deep in suds from washing dishes when her phone rang on the dining room table. She hollered, "Can you get that?"

"Got it," said Fen. He put the phone on speaker and announced, "Bailey Madison's answering service."

"Mr. Fen?"

It surprised him that Ren didn't giggle. "Yep."

"It's Ren. I need Bailey to come get me. Mom's at work and Dad thinks those two creeps pretending to be detectives will arrest him if he crosses the county line."

"I told Bailey I thought they might come early and wake your dad."

"You knew they'd do that?"

"It was an educated guess. Did they give him a hard time?"

"They tried to get him to say how many guns he owned. He asked why they wanted to know. They wouldn't give a straight answer, only that they were detectives and he needed to answer their questions. Dad then asked if they had search or arrest warrants. They kept answering his questions with ones of their own."

"That's not unusual. What happened next?"

"Things went downhill like a marble on a metal slide. Dad insisted they read him his rights before he'd consider answering questions. They kept threatening him with arrest. He wouldn't say anything except for them to get out of his house. That's when they looked at me and told me they were bringing me back to Georgetown. I told them I'd find my way without their help. That's when Dad called an attorney he knows."

"In their defense," said Fen, "the sheriff told them to bring you here as a favor to me. I'm guessing they didn't like the assignment."

"They also told Dad there was more than one way to get him to cooperate. What did they mean?"

Fen groaned. By this time, Bailey had dried her hands and was standing close to him with hands on hips and a scowl on her face. "They're bullies who don't like people who stand up to them. I'm leaving now to get you. Text me the address."

Bailey's truck shot out of the driveway and sped away in the general direction of Austin. Fen's plan of having the detectives do a favor for him proved to be an unmitigated disaster. He slumped into the recliner and looked up at the ceiling. A thought came from that unknown place where thoughts originate. Perhaps Bailey could salvage the interview with Robert. It was worth a shot.

The simple manipulation of his phone was all it took to get Bailey. His first words were, "Slow down and listen. I have an assignment for you and Ren."

"It's about time you gave me something to do. What is it?"

"Find out where Ren's father was the day his grandfather's house burned and what he was doing the night before last."

Bailey immediately asked, "You need his alibis?"

"Correct. Also, get a read on his relationship with his family, particularly his attitude toward his grandfather and father. Also, find out what he thinks about his brothers."

"Ren said he's not crazy about either of them. Les isn't too bad, but he thinks he's pretending to be a holy roller. As for Chance, he doesn't trust him."

"That's good information. Try to find out why he doesn't trust him. Also, ask if he thinks his father was ever married to Prissy."

"Anything else?"

"Yeah. Don't come back to Georgetown on I-35. Take a different route."

She dragged out her response of, "All right. Why not on the interstate?"

"I have a suspicion Ren hasn't seen the last of those detectives. They'll expect you to use the interstate."

"So what? I'll be doing the speed limit."

"It's not about how fast you're going. It's about them using Ren to get the information they want. If they can't get it out of her dad, they'll try to get it out of her."

"Ren knows every county road and back street in town. You know I can smell cop cars from a mile away. We'll make it back with no trouble."

"Don't get overconfident. Slow down and keep your wits about you. We can't afford any mistakes at this point."

"We must be getting close to the end of the investigation."

"Perhaps. One thing's for sure—it's not the time to make silly mistakes."

Fen sat in silence for at least fifteen minutes, considering the assignment he'd given Bailey. She was a bright young woman with more than her share of street smarts. She was also prone to overconfidence and trying too hard to prove herself. He wondered if he'd given her too big of an assignment. It was too late to second guess his decision.

Dismissing the thoughts, he rose and grabbed a sketch pad and artist pencils. Adonis needed his likeness captured for posterity before he slipped into doggy depression.

Chapter Twenty-Eight

It wasn't long before Fen pulled into Prissy's driveway. A new banner had joined the one promoting a cemetery for pets. This one was even bigger and bolder. It read GIVE GENEROUSLY TO THE PET CEMETERY FUND.

Fen stepped onto the porch and wondered if anyone ever bothered ringing the doorbell as the four-legged sentries made it superfluous. The barking started when he closed the door to his truck and continued until Prissy returned from rounding up the dogs and putting them in the fenced backyard.

"The children get so excited when company comes," said Prissy as the front door swung open. "Thanks for coming on such short notice. I thought Adonis would improve with the addition of another sister, but she didn't earn even a sniff. I believe the only thing that will bring him around is a framed drawing of his likeness. My praise of Donovan's sketch had him so upset."

Prissy cradled Adonis in her arms and motioned with her head for Fen to go into the living room. "I hope my call didn't interrupt your day. It's most generous of you to agree to come to my aid."

"Think nothing of it," said Fen. "You called at a good time. The paint from my morning session needs to dry before I add to it."

"What are you painting?"

"The San Gabriel, just down from the Highway 29 bridge. The one adjacent to the Duvant ranch."

Fen settled into a chair, as did Prissy, still clutching Adonis. She asked, "Speaking of the Duvant ranch, how is your investigation progressing?"

Fen shook his head. "I thought we were making progress, but it seems I've run into a brick wall. The sheriff has made it clear he no longer desires my help."

"Such a fool, but it doesn't surprise me. I've found him to be unresponsive to my complaints about cruelty toward animals. As you can see by my front yard, I'm quite active politically."

"I noticed the new banner. Did you form a non-profit in order to collect funds for the cemetery?"

"Of course. Someone should have done it years ago. I blame myself for not being more involved back then." She took in a deep breath. "Oh well, better late than never."

Fen flipped the sketch pad to a blank page. It was then he noticed he'd picked up Ren's pad in his haste to leave. "How do you want to pose Adonis?"

"Oh, dear," said Prissy. "I hadn't considered posing him. What's your recommendation?"

"He looks content and alert like he is. I can crop the top and bottom to show him in your arms but not your face or legs."

Excitement filled Prissy's response. "That sounds perfect. Make sure you don't show my face. He loves to be held but insists on living up to his name."

Faint lines appeared on the paper as Fen made confident strokes. He spoke as he worked. "Were you able to speak with Gil at the hospital, or did Sunny monopolize his time?"

"He and I are on cordial, but somewhat strained, terms. I find it best to communicate through Sunny."

Fen quirked his head to one side. "I thought your separation was amicable."

"It started off that way. He thinks I'm dragging my feet on agreeing to a divorce."

"Are you?"

It was Prissy's turn to tilt her head. "Such a direct question."

Fen held up a hand. "Sorry. Old habits are hard to break. I sometimes forget I'm no longer a sheriff."

Prissy spoke as she stroked Adonis. "I have nothing to hide. I'm delaying the divorce to give Sunny a chance to get to know Gil and all his quirks. She's ambitious, and so is he. I believe in the old saying of opposites attracting. In some ways, they're too similar, but in other ways, the differences are too significant. I'm afraid their marriage won't last long enough for the ink to dry on the marriage license."

Fen wondered about the response but agreed in principle that it was difficult for two hyper-ambitious people to share a life. In addition, there were decades between their ages. Then again, he wondered why Prissy had made it her business to try and manipulate the relationship.

Time passed as Fen took extra care to add details to the drawing. While he drew, Prissy rambled on about the pet cemetery. He lost interest somewhere between the physical layout and the crematorium.

One last check and he held it up for Prissy's inspection. He knew it was good and the reaction of Prissy and Adonis proved it. The dog's tail wagged like a metronome while Prissy gushed compliments.

Fen fanned through the sketch pad. "I owe you an apology. I grabbed the wrong sketch pad on my way out the door. Ren and Bailey will have to bring you the drawing of Donovan."

"Oh, dear. I was so hoping to have both sketches to frame. I'm still trying to improve Donovan's self-image and if he catches me fawning over Adonis, it may destroy his ego."

"I'll make sure Ren and Bailey deliver both together." On the way out, Fen glanced into the den. He hadn't noticed the gun case with glass doors. The sight froze him in place.

Prissy noticed his reaction and said, "It's all that's left of my greatest sin and shame. In my youth, I was an avid hunter." She motioned for him to enter.

He did so and looked into a case void of firearms.

It took no prompting for Prissy to expound. "Blood is on my hands. I murdered many defenseless animals, but I'm doing all I can to repent. This empty case reminds me not to waver in my commitment to atone for my sins."

Fen responded with a non-committal "Ah."

When Fen reached his truck, he noticed how much time had passed. His insistence on making the drawing something special had gobbled up over two hours. He wondered if Bailey and Ren had made it back.

Thick traffic slowed Fen's return to the rental but gave him time to mull over the case. It lasted until he pulled onto the street where they were staying and saw red and blue staccato lights flashing from the unmarked vehicle parked behind Bailey's truck.

He then noticed Lou's Camry in the driveway. She stood in the yard with her phone pointed toward Bailey. A man wearing street clothes had her leaned over the hood of the police car with handcuffs securing her wrists.

The man he knew to be the lead detective came to him. "That girl of yours has a smart mouth."

Instead of arguing, Fen gave a simple nod. "Is she under arrest?"

"We have her detained for our safety."

Another nod. He knew if she'd done something worthy of arrest, she'd be on her way to jail. "Other than the officer's safety, and the fact she has a habit of speaking what's on her mind, why is she detained?"

"That's none of your business."

"You're the one who approached me. If you don't want to talk to me, I'll go inside. By the way," He pointed to Lou. "That lady is a very well-known newspaper reporter. You'd better have a good reason for detaining Ms. Madison. I hear YouTube videos can wreck careers."

The double blink told Fen that his veiled threat had struck home. The detective responded with a terse question. "Where have you been today?"

Fen considered saying, "None of your business," but played it straight. "I had breakfast and some wonderful coffee at JUST LOVE early this morning. After that, I returned here and painted until noon. Then, I went to a lady's home and drew a pencil sketch of her dog. She was delighted with how it turned out, as was her dog."

The detective glared. "Now I know who the girl gets her smart mouth from."

"No, she came with that mouth as standard equipment."

"Hilarious. You won't be laughing if I catch you interfering in a police investigation."

Fen had heard all he could take. "Would that be the same investigation you botched six months ago or the one where I had to show you the bullet hole in Gil Duvant's truck?"

The detective ground his teeth.

"By the way," said Fen. "The reporter is standing right behind you. She's very light on her feet and now has everything you've said recorded. Unless you're going to detain me or Ms. Madison for telling the truth, I'd appreciate it if you released her and left this property. I don't think Sheriff Rhoads is in the mood for any more negative publicity caused by you."

Fen cast his gaze to the officer's car. "By the way, leave Ren Duvant here. Your plan to use her as leverage to get any weapons her father might own won't work. His attorney is waiting for you to make a mistake, and that would be a big one."

Faced with such a barrage of truth bombs, the detective turned and strode back to his vehicle. He spoke loud enough for Fen and Lou to hear, "Get the cuffs off her."

Fen stood by Lou, who kept filming until Ren exited the back seat and the car sped away from the curb. A wide smile pulled at the corners of Lou's mouth. "That felt so good." The smile disappeared. "Don't you dare tell me I can't do a story on this."

Fen ran a hand down his face. "Let me think about it."

"How long? There's a deadline to meet."

"Gather all the research you've done and give it to me. We also need to find out what Bailey discovered from her trip to see Ren's dad."

Lou pressed her lips together into a thin line before she said, "Then you'll spend all night reading every word. That means today's deadline will come and go." She huffed, "Why did I ever agree to do what you asked? I get juicy stories that could make me big bucks and have to sit on them."

Fen took all the slack out of his posture. "I've given you good stories and I'll keep doing it, but we're not here to carpet-bomb the cops." Fen lifted his chin. "Just so you know, that lead detective is beyond saving. The sheriff's looking for someone to blame, and he's painting a target on that guy as we speak. A day or two more and he'll be happy for you to write a story."

"Don't you need to solve the cases first?"

"I know what happened last summer and who killed Gilbert, but it's going to be hard to prove. It's the attempt to kill Gil that I'm struggling with."

"You were asked to help solve the murder. It seems the attempted murder is all on the shoulders of the sheriff."

"You're right, but I still think there's a link between the two. Besides, if I don't solve both, it will drive me nuts."

Bailey and Ren were waiting on the porch, where Ren performed one of her trademark spins with arms out. Lou chuckled as they joined them.

"That was kind of cool. I've never been in the back of a police car before. I didn't know the seats were hard plastic."

Fen pointed to the front door. "Thelma left us a tin of her tollhouse cookies with either chocolate or white chocolate chips. How does milk and a snack sound?"

Ren spun another circle. Bailey cracked up laughing and copied her spin move.

Chapter Twenty-Nine

Tall glasses of milk and a plate of Thelma's cookies put everyone in a better mood. Fen knew Bailey would give her opinion of the detective's actions, and she didn't disappoint. Thankfully, it was more of a summer dust devil and not a tornado.

A 'gnarly experience' was how Ren described being handcuffed.

A thought swept through Fen's mind about Bailey and Ren's friendship. For Bailey, friendships were few. Ren skipped through life, taking people as they were, liking most and tolerating all. Opposites were pulling the two together. Perhaps Bailey would someday move to Georgetown where she could be around like-minded artists.

Lou's question to Ren broke Fen's mental woolgathering. "It seems the detectives wanted access to any weapons your father might own. What did he tell them?"

Ren held a cookie in each hand, alternating between bites as her cheeks bulged. Bailey shook her head. "What are you doing?"

She chewed and swallowed. "I'm conducting a taste test. Can't decide if I like the dark chocolate or the white chocolate best." Her eyes opened wide like she'd discovered the cure to an exotic disease. "I know. Mix the two chocolates into the same batter and call it a two-for-one tollhouse cookie. Who says you have to choose between the two?"

Lou remarked, "You certainly think outside the box. If you can make Thelma believe it was her idea and talk her into giving you her batter recipe, you could become rich."

Ren waved a hand. "Nah. It would be too much work running a cookie company. I wouldn't have time to paint."

Lou changed the subject. "Back to my question about guns. What did your father tell them?"

"Oh, yeah. Sorry. He told them to come back with a search warrant, which would be a total waste of time. There's never been a gun of any kind in our house. I think it has something to do with Dad being a vegan."

Fen joined the conversation. "How long has he been a vegan?"

"Forever, as far as I know. He's cool about me eating burgers and hot dogs, but not in our house."

"It must have been tough on him growing up on a cattle ranch and not eating meat."

She shrugged. "I guess. He doesn't talk about it. Music is his life."

Bailey entered the conversation. "Ren told me on the way home that her dad had a three-day gig in San Antonio when her great-grandfather's house burned. He was playing in Austin when someone took a shot at her granddad. I have the names of the clubs if you want me to verify."

Lou piped up. "That's my specialty. I'll take care of it tonight."

Ren pushed away from the table. "That was my kind of

supper. My dad would be proud that I ate vegan." She looked at her glass of milk. "Well, almost vegan. Some people count dairy while others don't."

A knock on the front door caused everyone's eyes to shift in that direction. Lou asked, "Is anyone expecting company?"

Ren let out a laugh that sounded like the tinkling of a silver bell.

Bailey looked at the time on her phone. "He's early."

"Who?" asked Fen.

"Cory Blane. We're going to a movie."

The face and uniform of the deputy flashed in Fen's mind.

Ren volunteered the next bit of information. "I'm staying here and painting. They wanted me to go with them, but I could tell Cory has the hots for Bailey and didn't want me tagging along."

"It's just a movie, but one I've been wanting to see. No big deal."

Fen and Lou traded a quick glance but said nothing while Bailey went to the door. Muted words drifted into the dining room. Bailey's yell followed. "We're going for a burger before the movie starts. Bye."

The reporter in Lou kicked in. She tilted her head and asked, "How long has Cory been interested in Bailey?"

Fen shrugged but Ren had the answer. "Cory tried to hide it when we found Great-Grandpa's body, but I could tell. He was so tongue-tied he had to walk away from her. She thought he was a jerk until I told her he said she took his breath away. He's really sweet."

Lou pressed on. "What does she think about Cory being a deputy?"

"She said being around Fen has given her an appreciation for most cops. It's the bullies she can't stand. Cory is all business on the job but he's extra polite and patient with people."

Fen quipped, "He'll need a booster shot of patience if he's around Bailey for any length of time."

Lou stood. "You two probably want to paint. I'll clear the table and go to my room and knock out the story about Ren and Bailey being detained."

"Good idea," said Fen as he turned to Ren. "I accidentally picked up your sketch pad on my way out the door earlier today. I went to see Prissy to fulfill a promise I'd made her to draw Adonis."

Ren giggled. "It wasn't my sketch pad." She looked up and away. "Well, it was and wasn't mine. Bailey gave it to me." A note of seriousness entered her voice. "Would you mind looking at what I've done so far with the painting of Great-Grandpa and Great-Grandma? I'm having trouble with his ears."

"Sure. Those can be tricky because many people's ears aren't a perfect match."

They walked to the living room and both stood in front of her canvas. He gave a nod. "You have an excellent memory, perhaps too good. The mood of the painting is one of deep affection. You've done a great job of showing the joy of two elderly people reliving their early days of marriage. I can see it by the way they're dancing to the music of their youth. The old-school record player is a brilliant touch. Their facial expressions are good, especially hers with her eyes closed."

"Then why can't I figure out what's wrong with it?"

"You were right, it's his ears. They're too big."

"That's how they looked. He always had a buzz cut and elephant ears."

"Did he ever wear a hat or cap?"

"A John Deer baseball cap whenever he was outside, but not inside."

"Hmm," said Fen. "There are two things you can consider.

First, put a cap on him. The second is to make the ears smaller. It's all right to use artistic license in paintings. It's the mood and feelings you're trying to communicate. Otherwise, people would only want photographs."

Ren slapped herself on the forehead. "Of course. I have no trouble doing that in murals. The colors are super-vibrant and they depict bold actions and special events with all kinds of action."

Fen responded with a nod.

"I'll leave the hat off, but give him a little more hair and pin his ears back some. That should draw the eye away."

Fen took another look at the painting. "Is the dog Billy?"

"No. That's Bob but he looks so much like Billy, they could be twins. He was the Australian Shepherd I remember seeing photos of when I was growing up."

"He's having fun, watching them dance."

"Grandpa always loved his dogs. Only had one at a time, but they wouldn't hardly leave him. It took me a while to get Billy to go with me to the river."

Something niggled at Fen's brain, but it was like a small perch tugging on bait. The cork bobbed but wouldn't go under. He shook off the feeling and walked to his easel. Perhaps he could tease the thought back if he lost himself in his work-in-progress.

For the next two hours, he used every mental trick he knew to focus on the river and let it speak to him. Nothing came.

The scuffing of Lou's house shoes sounded before she appeared at the junction of the hall and the living room. She held a thick, brown file folder and announced, "Here's the research notes you wanted. I'll be in my room editing video. Are you going to eat anything for supper?"

Fen wagged his head. "Thelma's cookies took away any hunger pangs I might have had."

"Same with me. Will you wait up for Bailey?"

"I will," said Ren. "I want to hear if the movie is any good."

Fen gave her a sly smile. "That's not the only reason you're staying up. You want to know how her date turned out."

Ren turned her gaze toward her painting. "Of course. It's what girls our age do."

Fen looked at the lack of progress he'd made with his painting. It was one of those nights when the muse didn't show. He knew from experience that he could try to press through, but the results wouldn't be to his liking. Better to clean his brushes and do something else.

He carried the file folder into his bedroom, closed the door, and was soon sliding between the sheets on the king-size bed. Page by page, he reviewed the file while occasionally whispering rhetorical questions to Sally. He still counted on her to be a good listener and she never disappointed him. Slumber came like a cat wearing socks.

A shaft of sunlight stabbed his freshly opened eyes. He slammed them shut and realized sleep had overtaken him hours earlier. He turned over and oriented himself to the place, time, and why he was in a strange bed. The contents of the file folder spread across half the bed brought everything into focus. He'd been wondering what happened to Gilbert's dog, Billy.

The question about Billy's whereabouts continued to vex him as he brushed his teeth. Without warning, it was one of those bolt-out-of-the-blue moments. The piece to the jigsaw puzzle that fully explained Gilbert Duvant's murder fell into place.

A word of caution swept over him. It was one thing to know who killed Gilbert and why. It was another thing to prove it.

Chapter Thirty

The coffee pot gurgled and then sputtered out the last drops. Fen made it stronger than usual to ensure an active mind, not only for himself but for those who would join him at the breakfast table. The outline of a plan to catch Gilbert's killer was jelling. Not so much with the second crime against Gil.

Lou was the first to join him. The dark circles under her eyes told the tale of a late night of writing and editing.

Even though his thoughts danced with ideas of how to bring the cases to a successful conclusion, he waited until Lou broke the ice. Her first words came when she looked up from a half-empty cup. "Stay up late?" she asked.

"I'm not sure. It was after midnight but before six-fifteen this morning."

"Do you know who killed Gilbert Duvant and tried to kill Gil?"

He answered with a slow nod. "Yes, to the first. Almost sure, to the second."

Lou stiffened. "You have my attention."

"Good. I'm going to need a lot of help to prove their guilt."

"What can I do?"

"We need to get Bailey and Ren out of the house. I'm going to call the sheriff and ask him to come over. The first thing I need to do is get his lead detective out of the way. That's where you come in. Do you have the video ready to show the sheriff?"

"I didn't go to sleep until I edited it."

"Did you keep the raw footage?"

"Of course."

"Good. That's all I want him to see. I want any discipline that the detectives experience to be Stony's idea and without your commentary."

"Are you saying I can't post it?"

"Only with his permission."

Lou's throat mottled with crimson as anger seemed to rise from the neck of her robe. "The next thing you're going to tell me is I can't be present when the arrests take place."

Fen gave only a slight shake of his head and spoke in a soft tone. "You'll be there, but I need leverage to get the sheriff to agree. That means trading your video to get him to go along with my plan."

"Are you saying there will be more than one arrest?"

"One for sure. More than one if we get lucky."

Lou leaned back as she seemed to weigh her options. "I'll do it your way, but it's under protest."

They both sipped coffee until her pinched eyebrows told him a question had worked its way into Lou's mind and would soon pass her lips. Nothing new about that. Lou's journalism background ensured a steady stream of questions. The words came out fast. "You said we need to get Bailey and Ren out of the house while you wheel and deal with the sheriff. Is that the only reason?"

Fen's lips parted in a sly smile. "Ren will play a vital part in my plan. I want her actions and reactions to be organic."

"Let me get this straight," said Lou as she raised her index finger. "First, you manipulate me into not doing my job as a reporter." She held up a thumb. "Next, you're going to manipulate the sheriff. I won't hold that one against you because I think the chief detective needs to retire." Her middle finger joined the other two. "Third, you're putting things in place to get Ren to do something she normally wouldn't do if she knew what it was. How many other deceptions can I expect?"

Fen spoke in a somber tone with his gaze fixed on Lou. "As many as it takes to keep Gil Duvant alive."

Bailey and Ren made their not-so-grand appearance a short time later. Fen hovered over the stove as Bailey came and poured a cup of coffee. She took one sip and asked, "Did you make this?"

"Yeah. Good, huh?"

"It'll sure wake me up."

Fen knew his next question was none of his business, but he asked anyway. "How was your date with Cody?"

"I thought we agreed you wouldn't butt into my personal life."

He held up his hands. "Just asking. It must have been pretty lousy if you're going to bite my head off."

Bailey exaggerated the raising of her chin and spoke in an aristocratic tone. "Mr. Blane was a true gentleman and Miss Madison behaved with exemplary decorum."

Fen turned back to the stove and stirred the scrambled eggs. "Serves me right for asking."

He waited a few seconds. "I have an assignment for you and Ren this morning."

"We wanted to paint."

"You can do that this afternoon. We need research done on

the history of the county, especially on the places we're painting. Focus on the San Gabriel when you go to the library."

Bailey shook her head. "This sounds like a homework
assignment I had to do in the tenth grade. What's the use?"

He turned off the heat and took down a platter. "When we
do the gallery exhibition this summer, people will ask us about
our choice of scenes along the river. Sales is about connecting
with the patrons. If you can throw out a handful of facts about
the site you painted or something about history, it will go a long
way to building rapport."

"History is so boring," countered Bailey.

Fen countered her statement with a question. "Who's
Three-Legged-Willie, and why is he important to Williamson
County?"

Ren chose that moment to come into the kitchen. "I know.
There's a statue of him in front of the museum downtown,
across from the courthouse. He really had three legs."

"No way," said Bailey.

"I'll show you," said Ren. "I heard you talking about the
library. There's a room upstairs dedicated to local stuff and
there's a nice cafe downstairs. Yummy pastries. Mr. Fen's right
about schmoozing with customers. The murals I paint are all
about history. It really helps to know about the location and
events that happened there."

Bailey held up her hands in surrender. "Fine. We'll go to
the library and find out all about some old dude with three
legs."

"Focus on the river, too," said Fen. "That's going to be the
theme of our gallery show."

"All right. We'll go."

Fen breathed a soft sigh of relief. He'd accomplished one of
the day's goals. The next might be more difficult. He wondered
how the sheriff would react.

Sheriff Rhoads arrived five minutes after eleven that morning. He wasn't smiling. Fen tried to brighten the mood. "I hope you don't mind if we talk at the dining room table. As you can see, we've turned the living room into a makeshift art studio."

It came as a bit of a surprise that the sheriff didn't stop to look at any of the three paintings. All he said was, "There better not be any paint on the floor, or Sunny Day will bill your credit card for an extra cleaning fee."

Lou was quick to ask, "Have you had dealings with her before?"

"She's a tough businesswoman who won't hesitate to call us if there's damage to a rental."

It wasn't what he said, but the tone of the sheriff's words that told Fen he'd caught the sheriff in a rotten mood. Perhaps one of Thelma's cookies would help lubricate their conversation.

Lou shot him a glance with one eyebrow rising above the other. It was her way of asking a question without words. Fen nudged his head toward the hallway. She nodded and retreated to her bedroom. They'd agreed ahead of time that if either of them sensed the sheriff didn't want her present, she'd disappear and let him do the talking.

Fen didn't ask if the sheriff wanted coffee and a snack. He simply went to the kitchen, where a fresh pot stood at the ready. He poured two mugs, placed them on the table, and retrieved a plate of cookies.

Stony bypassed both coffee and cookies, preferring to get down to business. "If you don't know who killed Gilbert Duvant, I'm leaving. I've had a rotten day, and it has all the makings of getting worse."

Fen delayed responding by raising his mug to his lips and blowing the steam away. This gave Stony time to consider his sharp words and keep talking. "Sorry. I suspended my lead detective this morning. The city's chief of police drove by during yesterday's stop of Ren Duvant and your protégé. The stop wasn't called in."

"Ah," said Fen as he put his mug on the table. "That's a serious breach of protocol. Did you suspend both of them?"

"Only the one. He was calling the shots." Stony cast a questioning eye at him. "Why haven't I seen a YouTube video on the stop and detainment yet? I know your reporter filmed everything."

Fen motioned toward the far end of the house. "I told Lou to hold off until after I spoke with you."

"Is she going to?"

"She'll keep it to herself if you allow her to be present when you arrest Gilbert Duvant's killer."

Pinched eyebrows matched the next question. "Do you know who killed Gilbert?"

Fen gave his head a slow nod.

"Do you know who tried to kill Gil?"

Another nod, but it came with qualifying words. "I'm ninety-nine percent sure about that one."

"Can you prove it?"

"With your help, we'll get one for sure."

"What can I do?"

Fen rubbed his chin. "Several things. Have a cookie and I'll write out a list."

Fen wrote while the sheriff took a tentative bite, followed by a full one.

"Where did you get these cookies?"

"My housekeeper and cook made them."

Stony's shoulders dipped a quarter of an inch as worries

seemed to thaw. He finished the cookie and reached for seconds. "This day is turning out better than it started." He took another bite and spoke after he swallowed. "Yes, sir, much better than it started."

The sound of Stony leaving was Lou's signal to come out of her room. She stepped into the living room as Fen approached his painting. "Well?" she asked. "Am I invited to the big party?"

"You'll be there from beginning to end. Stony will make sure all the suspects are there."

"Where's there?"

"At Gil's home on the Duvant ranch. Deputies will make sure everyone comes."

"Everyone?"

Fen nodded but added, "Not at the same time. The timing is going to be tricky, but if we do it right, we should solve both crimes."

"Are you going to tell me your plan?"

A mischievous smile came to Fen. "Your part will be to capture audio and video. You and I will arrive in plenty of time to set up a couple of your miniature cameras and do sound checks."

Lou wiggled her eyebrows and smiled, then smoothed her features and asked, "Why do I have the feeling you're not going to tell me your plan?"

"It will make a better story for you if I don't." He stared at his painting. "Besides, everything could blow up in my face."

Lou took a step toward her bedroom. "That might make an even better story."

Chapter Thirty-One

It was the calm before the storm, and Fen knew it would test his patience. It wasn't long before Lou announced her plan of going to the library and spending the rest of the day studying the history of the county.

That left Fen with the afternoon by himself. He spent it making slow, deliberate brush strokes of oils on canvas, adding depth and details to his painting of the San Gabriel. For the first time since he arrived, he slipped into the flow of painting. It freed his mind to review the facts of the case. His plan was good but not foolproof.

Afternoon turned into evening and then night. All the women returned to the nest, and the foursome enjoyed one of the remaining meals Thelma had prepared for them. The light banter throughout the meal made for an enjoyable gathering at the table.

After the kitchen was clean, the two young artists joined Fen to work on their paintings. A little after ten, he washed out his brushes and bid them goodnight.

Unlike most cases, he put all thoughts of the Duvant

murder and attempted murder to sleep as he whispered good-night to Sally. It was after seven the next morning before he pushed back the covers.

The phone call from Sheriff Rhoads came a few minutes before eleven that morning. He'd arranged everything. Deputies would ensure the arrival of all suspects at the agreed-upon times.

Ren was on the front porch giving a daily report to her mother. They spoke every day before her mom took her lunch break. Fen used the quiet to take a major step toward solving the crimes. He rested his brushes in a cup of solvent and directed his words to Bailey. "I need to talk to you about some-thing very important. Meet me in the backyard."

He'd used his cop voice. It wasn't something he did often with her, and it had the desired effect. She immediately thrust her brush into her own jar of solvent and followed him. They walked in silence until they reached the middle of the yard.

"I have a very special assignment for you this evening. The timing of it needs to be perfect, and what I want you to do is going to be almost illegal."

She took a step back, but the shock of his words quickly faded. "This sounds like it could be fun."

"I'm going to send you to the house of one of the suspects. You're to retrieve something from the backyard of the home. There's a chain link fence you'll need to go through or get over. I'm not sure if there's a lock on the gate or not."

Fen gave her details that included the address, what she was retrieving, and where she was to come.

"What if someone asks me what I'm doing?"

"Get creative and use your best judgment."

This brought on a full smile.

"Listen carefully. You're going to be on a tight timeline. Cory will receive a call to do a welfare check at the residence I gave you. Be sure you're not in the backyard or in the house when he arrives." He gave her his best no-nonsense look. "Will you do this?"

"No problem. Ren and I can be gone in less than three minutes."

"Ren will be with me at her grandfather's home. You and Cory will have something like a second date, but this one will be in his patrol car. You'll leave your truck there."

"Cool. It will be different to ride in the front seat. All my rides as a juvie were in the back seat."

"One more thing," said Fen. "What's going to happen this evening will be hard on Ren. She can't know about it, so you have to wear a poker face until it's over."

"Is she in trouble?"

Fen shook his head. "No, but someone she loves will be."

Bailey swallowed. "I don't like this part of investigating murders."

"Neither do I, but it's what I do."

She corrected him. "It's what we do."

Ren was already at her easel when they shuffled back into the living room. She was so absorbed in her painting that she didn't ask about their meeting. All three passed the day painting different scenes.

The call from Stony came a few minutes after five; later than expected. Fen answered it by stating his name.

"Everything's still on track," said Stony and the call ended.

Fen pretended the sheriff was still talking. He responded with, "Yes, Ren's here." An extended pause followed. "I understand. We're on our way."

The sheriff's name disappeared from Fen's phone. "That was Sheriff Rhoads. He wants me, Lou, and Ren to get to Gil's home as soon as possible. He says he knows who killed Ren's great-grandfather, and he wants all the family to hear it at the same time."

Ren looked at Bailey. "I want you to go with me."

Fen hadn't planned for this, but Bailey helped him out by asking, "Did he say he wanted me to come?"

Fen responded by wagging his head. He quickly added. "He told me he wanted Lou there to make sure there was a seasoned reporter to write the story. I'm going because I helped him put together some clues."

Bailey quickly added, "Don't worry about me, Ren. I'm used to getting left out."

Lou and Ren waited on Fen to trade his house shoes for boots. He figured it would take fifteen minutes to reach the front gate of the Duvant ranch and another four or five before he pulled into Gil's driveway. He parked the truck and checked the time. He'd missed the estimate by forty-five seconds.

Ren led the way and didn't bother knocking. They entered through the garage and walked through the kitchen, where a woman with graying hair met Ren with a two-armed hug. Fen guessed she was Gil's housekeeper and cook, the Hispanic version of Thelma. Her greeting to Ren also told him the woman enjoyed the status of almost-family.

After introductions, Ren asked, "Where's Grandpa?"

"In the den. Much pain, so he takes pills and sleeps." She shooed her with her hands. "Go see him. He's expecting you."

They passed through what Fen would describe as the great room. The size looked to be half of a basketball court with dark hardwood floors. The room seemed to swallow the leather, overstuffed furniture and tables that displayed a variety of bronze statues. It was the room a visitor would see first when they came through the front door. The statement it made was, "I'm rich and proud of it."

They traveled down a hall until Ren turned and led them

into a room with more reasonable dimensions and furniture that looked like it wanted whoever sat on it to be comfortable. The exuberant granddaughter made a straight line for Gil and took his hand in hers. "Grandpa, you have company."

Eyelids flickered open. Gil licked his lips. His voice cracked when he said, "Hello, little bird. I see you've brought the lawman and the reporter."

"Former lawman," said Fen. "How are you feeling, Mr. Duvant?"

"Like a bull used my chest for a dance floor." He took a shallow breath. "What time is it?"

"Not yet five-thirty."

"The sheriff said the party wouldn't start for another hour."

"That's correct. Lou needs to set up a couple of tiny cameras."

Gil turned his head and gave Lou a thorough once-over. "She's a lot better looking than the night shift nurses at the hospital."

Ren squeezed his hand. "Behave yourself, Grandpa. In case you don't remember, there's one woman who says she's still married to you and another who says she's going to marry you."

Gil's eyelids drooped. "That don't stop me from looking and flirtin' a little." He looked at Lou and winked.

Lou came back with, "I'll make a deal with you, Mr. Duvant. You look all you want, and I'll set up a couple of cameras."

The next thing out of Gil's mouth was the expulsion of a breath as he drifted off to sleep.

"Just my luck," said Lou. "Another snorer. Two out of three of my former husbands could wake the dead."

"What was wrong with the other one?" asked Ren.

"He talked in his sleep. I wouldn't have minded it if it had been my name he called."

Fen cast his gaze to Ren, who was covering her mouth to stifle a giggle. "We have some time to kill. I noticed a big barn not too far from here. Could you show it to me?"

"Sure. That's where Grandpa keeps his prize bulls."

As usual, she was ready to go. He thought about the pet name Gil had given his granddaughter. She spelled her name REN, whereas he'd meant WREN, a small bird that flitted about. The nickname suited her.

Once outside, she asked, "Who's coming to the gathering?"

Fen named them off. "The sheriff, your parents, your two uncles, and Aunt Prissy."

"And you think one of them killed Great-Grandpa?"

"I'm afraid so."

"I hope you're wrong."

Chapter Thirty-Two

The sinking sun set the western sky ablaze with hues that ranged from violet to crimson. Fen and Ren talked about the colors as they made their way back from viewing livestock. Everything about the ranch was first-rate, and the bulls lived up to their billing as prize winners. A stab of envy hit him, but it was short-lived. What his bulls lacked in stature and pedigree, they made up for with enthusiasm and consistency. His much smaller herd produced sound, healthy calves that brought better-than-average prices at auctions. He quickly replaced covetousness with contentment.

As they neared the house, Fen saw two pickup trucks in the driveway that weren't there when he arrived. Ren provided the names of the trucks' owners. "Uncle Chance and Uncle Les are here." She looked down the gravel road. "That's Mom's Prius. Wouldn't it be cool if Dad was with her?"

She didn't have to wait long for an answer and hopped from one foot to the other when she identified the driver and passenger. "It's Dad! I can't believe he came to see Grandpa. This is so outstandingly awesome!"

Fen stood still as Ren ran to the passenger side of the car and waited for her father to step out. He was taller than expected, with hair pulled back into a ponytail and a patch of long whiskers on his chin that resembled the under-jaw beard of a goat. Blue jeans, slip-on shoes without socks, and a Grateful Dead T-shirt covered his lean frame. It was obvious he'd given up on the boots and Wrangler jeans of his upbringing.

Ren leaped into his open arms. "I can't believe you came to see Grandpa."

His voice sounded rich and full when he replied, not unusual for someone who made his living singing and playing a guitar. "That hick sheriff called my attorney. My lawyer told me to come, but I'm not to say a word."

Ren turned to Fen. "Is that right, Mr. Fen? Dad doesn't have to say anything?"

"Not a word unless he wants to. I'll let both of you in on a secret. Nothing bad is going to happen to your father tonight."

Ren's mother joined her husband and daughter. "Then why were we strong-armed into coming?"

"You can blame me. I didn't want you to get a second-hand report from Ren about tonight's meeting. Sometimes things get lost in recounting important events."

Ren grabbed her mother's hand and swung it back and forth. "He's saying I see things differently than most people. I don't like to tell all the yucky stuff."

June cupped her daughter's chin with her free hand. "And that's what makes you so special."

The sheriff's SUV came to a stop behind Fen's truck. He gave a nod to everyone but spoke only to Fen. "Are you ready to get this show on the road?"

"We're still missing people, but we can get started without them."

The sheriff adjusted his gun belt. "Prissy's on her way. By the time you finish your little speech, all but one will be here."

With that said, the gathering walked into Gil's home... all that is, except Ren. She skipped like a child without a care in the world.

They arrived in the den and interrupted a conversation between Gil and his eldest son, Chance. Les sat in a chair far enough away that he wasn't taking part in the conversation. Robert, the youngest son, led the way to a couch where he settled between his wife and daughter. Lou had already chosen a wingback chair with a view of the entire room. Fen and the sheriff stood in front of the fireplace, facing the room's occupants.

The sheriff kicked things off. "There's still a few more people who'll join us, but Fen Maguire isn't one to waste time. Some of you might wonder why I've called you here. There's a murder and an attempted murder to solve, and Sheriff Maguire was called on to do that very thing." He cast a piercing gaze around the room. "Someone that will be in this room tonight will leave wearing handcuffs."

The sheriff stepped aside and Fen took his place in front of the fireplace. Before he could say a word, June Duvant, Ren's mother, interrupted. "What authority does a former sheriff have in conducting a police investigation?"

Stony took two steps toward Fen. "He's a licensed private investigator with twenty-plus years in law enforcement. He's here because I needed help in unraveling a case I thought was closed. He and his team have been hard at work assisting me. To be more specific, Sheriff Maguire is still a certified law enforcement officer who's working under my authority." He faced June. "Does that answer your question?"

She answered with a nod.

Stony moved back to the side.

Fen took in a deep breath. "I want to begin by saying the murder of Gilbert Duvant was almost a perfect crime. At first, Gil wanted to move on quickly, but had second thoughts after the will was read. However, there wasn't a shred of evidence that suggested homicide or suicide until Ren and a fellow artist stumbled upon Gilbert's grave."

Fen continued. "Even though arson investigators found no traces of accelerants in the remains of Gilbert's home, Gil pressed on until I was asked to look into the case. What I initially found was a striking lack of evidence. The fire burned so hot that only ashes remained. The remote location and late hour delayed the fire department. There was no positive I.D. of a body."

"Why couldn't the coroner identify the body?" asked June.

"They found human ashes, but there was no chance of DNA analysis from them. The fire burned way too hot to preserve anything but tiny pieces of bone and dust."

"What about the teeth?"

Chance spoke for the first time. "What teeth? Grandpa hasn't had his teeth for years."

Fen summarized. "There was nothing to identify the body. It wasn't until Ren told us about Gilbert keeping his wife's ashes in the house that I realized the ashes they found likely belonged to her."

"She didn't have any teeth, either," said Ren.

The sheriff's phone dinged. He looked at the screen, then sent a text.

Fen cast a gaze at those assembled. "One more person will join us shortly, but we need to move on. The discovery of Gilbert's body added several things to the file folder, but not enough to convict anyone. When that happens, we look at motive."

One by one, he locked his gaze on each family member

then settled on Gil. "I ruled Gil out as the killer because of his father's advanced age. He knew nature would soon take its course."

Chance scoffed, "Grandpa was tough as an old boot and had at least ten more years in him."

Mumbles of agreement sounded around the room. Fen spoke over them. "I also ruled Gil out after I learned how wealthy he is in his own right. His other businesses give him plenty of money to live however he wants. He'd already given over control of the cattle to Chance, which showed me he wasn't ruled by the need to control."

No one had anything to say about this, so Fen moved on. "However, there is something we can't lose sight of."

He remained quiet until June said, "Don't keep us in suspense. What can't we lose sight of?"

"No one here could benefit financially from Gilbert's death except Gil, but everyone in this room could become wealthy if both Gilbert and Gil were dead." He pointed to Gil. "Look at him. Someone almost wiped out two generations in a little over six months."

The silence lasted for seconds as family members cast furtive gazes at each other. Chance was the first to speak. "There's someone who isn't here that we should consider."

"Oh? Who's that?"

"Sunny Day."

"Why Sunny?"

"She started calling me a year ago. She wants to buy Duvant land. And now she's dating Dad."

Gil sat up straight and let out a loud moan. With a hand clutching his side, he demanded, "Why didn't you tell me?"

Chance held up his hand to block the harsh words. "I didn't tell you because I knew it would set you off."

"You'd sell if you could, wouldn't you?"

Chance didn't back down. "I know how much the land means to you. I told her any selling of land would be your decision to make."

Gil narrowed his gaze. "You've been on me to sell half of it for some time."

Fen broke in. "Every one of Gil's sons could benefit from a double murder, but I believe none of you are responsible. Chance is happy to live life as it is. Les and Robert wouldn't mind a windfall, but they've both found peace living life in different ways."

"Amen to that," said Les.

Robert broke his silence by saying, "Right on."

Gil cast his gaze to his sons. "It seems Mr. Maguire has narrowed down the suspects to Sunny Day."

Fen gave his head a slow shake.

June sighed in frustration. "Is Sunny guilty or not?"

Fen let a few seconds tick by. "I have a plan that will prove the killer's guilt, but I'll need everyone's help to pull it off. Sheriff Rhoads needs everyone to take a permission form. It says they'll allow officers to look for firearms in their homes."

"No way!" said Robert.

Fen followed the objection with, "I didn't say they're going to conduct the search. You don't have to sign your name to them, only be prepared to hold them up when I tell you to. We want it to appear as if you're all agreeing to the searches."

June raised her eyebrows. "Aren't you the clever hound? You're counting on someone not agreeing to have their home searched."

Fen shrugged. "For this to work, you're all going to have to trust me, the sheriff, and Gil. Follow our lead."

A text alert came from Fen's phone. Bailey's name appeared.

We're here with a passenger. Mission accomplished.

He texted back.

Stay where you are until I tell you to come in.

The sheriff was the next to speak. "Officers are pulling up with our next guest."

Chapter Thirty-Three

Sunny Day jerked her arm from the officer's grasp as she stepped into the room. Her eyes flashed with anger as she focused on Stony Rhoads. "I don't appreciate being kidnapped!"

He spoke to the deputies escorting her. "Take the cuffs off." His next words went to Sunny. "You're being detained until our investigation is complete. The cuffs will go back on if you try to leave."

Fen took over and spoke in a softer tone. "I apologize for the inconvenience, but there's been some serious accusations made and we want to hear your side."

"I'm not saying anything without an attorney."

Gil spoke up. "Sugar, if what we've heard about you is true, you'll need a whole stable of lawyers."

Sunny glared at him. "What have you heard, and who said it?"

Gil dragged a palm down his face that looked as if he hadn't shaved for three days. "I'm hearing words to the effect that you had something to do with killing my father and taking a shot at me." His next words came in a rush. "I don't believe a word of it, but we need to get ahead of this before that crazy Prissy ruins your reputation with cheap talk."

Gil's story was good. Sunny batted her eyes at him. Was it to hold back a tear? Fen didn't think so.

"I can't believe this is happening to me," she whimpered.

"Trust me on this, sugar," said Gil. "We can settle everything quickly. I'll give you some land for your trouble."

Gil had gone off script and Fen tried not to allow his surprise to show. He'd called Gil earlier, gave him a report of Sunny's ongoing affair with developer Bart Hill, and solicited his help in unraveling the two crimes. They hadn't discussed trading a promise of land for Sunny's cooperation, but Fen was willing to let it play out and see where it went.

At the mention of free land, Sunny treated Gil with a coy smile. She then asked for details. "How many acres and where are they?"

"Five hundred. The location is up for discussion, but not within a half-mile of the river bottom."

Chance nodded his approval.

Judging by the smile that lit up Sunny's face, if there hadn't been a roomful of witnesses, Fen suspected she would have been in Gil's lap showing her appreciation.

Gil pointed to his eldest son. "You and Chance work out the location and other details. In fact, why don't you two go to my office and do that right now?"

"Are you sure, Dad?" asked Chance.

"It's time, son. Negotiate the way I taught you."

Fen's mind kicked into high gear as Chance and Sunny cleared the room. Gil's version of the plan had added an element of safety. With Sunny out of the room, they didn't have to worry about Gil, or anyone else for that matter, being caught in the crosshairs of a cat fight between two very conniving women. The new, revised plan meant he could take his time in getting leverage over Prissy. His next moves would make or break the case.

Sheriff Rhoads looked at Fen. "Are you ready for our next guest?"

"Ready when you are."

A short time later, Prissy was escorted in by a deputy, with Adonis cradled in her arms. She took in the room's occupants and said, "Isn't this cozy? No one told me we were having a family reunion."

Fen extended a hand toward an empty loveseat. "Please, make yourself comfortable."

She looked at the sheriff. "I should have known you're responsible for this. I'll be filing a formal complaint for abducting me from my home."

"You can blame me," said Fen. "We were discussing a near-perfect crime. Since you claim to be family, I thought it only right that you hear who killed your late father-in-law."

She cast her gaze to Gil, who wore a bathrobe over pajamas and sat still as a statue. "It should be obvious who had the most motive to want Gilbert dead. I'm surprised Gil hasn't sold some of the land to a housing developer already."

Fen ignored her attack on Gil. "I saw you speaking with Sunny at the hospital. My guess is you were asking her questions about Gil's accident." He put air quotes around the word accident.

"How did you know I was trying to discover what Sunny had done?"

"It wasn't you, but Sunny, who gave it away. She was way too intense with what you were saying, plus she wasn't interested in Gil's condition after she knew he'd live."

Prissy lifted her chin a fraction. "You *are* a clever man. I wanted to see how she'd react when I asked if she killed a deer this last season. She said she did, right here on the ranch."

"That's true," said Gil. "Killed a nice twelve-point the first week of December."

Prissy reacted with a shiver. "So barbaric. That proves she's a killer."

She opened her mouth to continue, but Fen cut her off. "What else did you ask her?"

"I asked what make and caliber of rifle she used for hunting. Sunny said it's a Stevens 308, with a 3 to 9 variable scope."

Fen had to hand it to Prissy. She'd thought long and hard about her story to implicate Sunny.

Stony took his turn. "That could be enough to get a search warrant, but things aren't like they used to be. Judges are requiring more proof to justify a warrant these days. Sometimes eliminating suspects who have strong motives can persuade a judge. We've passed out consent-to-search forms to all of Gil's sons."

Les held up his form. "Robert and I have agreed to allow them to search our homes for weapons. So has Chance."

It was a stretch of the truth, but it wasn't illegal and wasn't entrapment.

"Hand me one of those forms," said Prissy. "I've nothing to hide."

Stony handed her a form with details already filled in and waited as she scribbled her name.

Fen then said, "That should take care of the attempted murder, but there's one more. How long have you suspected Sunny of killing your father-in-law?" He purposefully used the title of father-in-law.

A look of superiority came across Prissy's countenance. "It's common knowledge that she's after land and doesn't much care how she gets it. Why else would she trick Gil into marrying her? Can't you see? She killed Gilbert and then tried to kill Gil. She knows Chance wants to sell half the land. With his dad out of the way, she knew he would sell to her."

Fen nodded. "You make a convincing argument, but you claim to still be married to Gil. That would have made you the heir if she'd killed Gil."

"What's one more murder to a woman like her? I'd be next."

Fen took out his drawing of an Australian Shepherd and showed it to Ren. "Study this carefully."

Ren took her time. "Wow. This is fantastic... so lifelike."

"Do you recognize the dog?"

"Of course. It's Billy."

"Let me see that," said Prissy.

Fen walked closer to Prissy and held up the drawing.

"Don't be silly. That's Donovan. Mr. Maguire drew it at my request."

Fen sent a text to Bailey while Ren insisted the drawing was of Gilbert's companion, Billy. "I know it's Billy because he had one ear with a small notch near the top. You can see it very plainly."

"Give it here," demanded Prissy. "I want to see it closer."

Stony intervened. "Prissy, that drawing is evidence. These deputies will use whatever force is necessary to make sure you don't touch it."

Bailey and Cory interrupted the scene as they arrived with Billy, AKA Donovan, walking between them. The dog looked around the room and went to Gil.

"Hello, Billy. Where have you been? Good to see you, old friend."

After strokes and ear rubs, Billy went to Prissy, who pretended not to know him. "Get away, mutt."

The dog's tilted head signaled confusion. He then went to Ren and received more strokes of affection.

Fen looked at Prissy. "Including Chance, there will be three family members who will swear this is Billy. Like Gilbert, the fire didn't kill Billy because he stayed at Gilbert's side like a second shadow. Neither of them were in the house when it exploded and began to burn. That leaves us with big questions for you, Prissy. How did you get Billy? If he survived the fire, why is he living at your home? And why did you give him a new name?"

"I can give a likely answer to those questions," said Stony. "She went to the ranch earlier that day, took Gilbert for a ride, killed him, and buried him in the soft soil near the river. As for Billy, she's the biggest animal lover in the county. Couldn't bring herself to kill him."

Prissy looked from Stony to Fen, but no words of defense came forth. It seemed she had been struck dumb.

Bailey cast her gaze to Prissy. "I stopped by your home and found the front door cracked open."

Cory added, "We received an anonymous call for a welfare check. Bailey was in the front yard with Billy when I arrived."

Prissy sputtered something under her breath that sounded like, "You're lying." Her voice rose in pitch. "I always lock my door."

Bailey shrugged. "Then someone must have broken in. I bet that's why the cops received a call for a welfare check."

"I'd believe that if I was serving on a jury," said Fen. He turned to Prissy. "If you're wondering how we know so much about what you did the day Gilbert died, you can thank your accomplice."

"What do you mean?"

Stony said, "It means Sunny likes to talk."

The sheriff then pointed to Cory. "You're the closest to her. Cuff Prissy and get her out of here."

The words hung in the air like a muddy, wet towel on a clothesline. But Prissy suddenly found her words and wasn't going down alone. "Wait. Look at me. Do I look like I could dig a grave by myself? And I don't know the first thing about gas heaters or stoves. Sunny does property management and knows all about stoves and how they work." She gasped for half a breath. "I don't own a pistol."

Fen countered with, "Are you saying all you did was help dig the grave?"

She nodded hard enough for her hair to fall in her face. "Sunny's the one who owns guns. I gave up on killing a long time ago."

"What kind of gun did she kill Gilbert with?"

"A .22 revolver. It only took one shot in the back of the head. She wanted to kill Billy, but I told her she'd have to kill me first. For a minute I thought she would."

The sheriff shook his head. "It's going to be her word against yours. You'd better come up with something else."

Prissy looked at the ceiling. Words followed as her gaze came down. "She threw the pistol in the river near where we buried him."

Fen took over. "That's a good start, but she'll say you threw it there."

Her eyes shifted as if she was looking for something to save her. "Tools! She carried a small toolbox with her. Used it to rig the space heater that caused the fire. She said she discovered how to delay the explosion on the Internet."

"That helps a lot," said Fen. "It might be enough to get Sunny a life sentence. Did you record any of your phone conversations when you two planned this?"

"I didn't think about it, but I wouldn't put it past Sunny.

She's a very detail-oriented person. All I could think about was finally getting land for my pet cemetery. Sunny promised me all the land I wanted to make my dream come true."

Fen nodded to Stony. "If the bullet you recovered from Gil's crash site matches Sunny's deer rifle, you'll get two convictions."

Stony gave Cory a firm nod. "Take Prissy to jail, Deputy Blane."

"What do you want me to charge her with?"

"Book her in for stealing a dog and suspicion of murder. I'll talk to the D.A. and add other charges tomorrow."

After Deputy Blane escorted Prissy from the room, Fen spoke to Les. "Would you mind telling Chance and Sunny they can complete their deal later? We have something we need to clear up with Sunny."

When everyone was once again settled, Fen addressed Sunny. "Do you recognize the dog?"

"Should I?"

"He's the dog you should have put in Gilbert Duvant's home before you rigged the gas to malfunction. We understand you discovered how on the Internet and you carry tools with you. The sheriff will have deputies in your home with search warrants tonight."

A smoldering gaze met his words.

"We also understand you threw the .22 pistol in the river near where you and Prissy tried to bury Gilbert. Divers will find it in the morning."

Fen had hoped that last revelation would turn on the spigot of confession. As he watched Sunny clench her teeth and the fire in her eyes diminish, he knew she was giving in for the moment.

Gil held his side and said, "It's time for the truth, Sunny."

"For a woman of detail, you really made at least three big mistakes," Fen said.

Ren looked at her fingers. "She threw the gun in the river and she didn't kill Billy. What's the third?"

Fen shifted his gaze from Fen to Sunny. "Choosing a ditsy partner like Prissy to help you. You should have known she'd sell you down the river to try and save herself."

Sunny remained mute. Fen suspected there was more to this story that hadn't been uncovered, but was convinced they wouldn't hear it tonight.

Stony nodded to a deputy. "Take her to jail."

"The same charges?"

"Nope. Murder and attempted murder."

With the killers revealed, the tension in the room released like water breaching a dam. Chance, Les and Robert remained in their seats. They looked as if they had something to say, but the words wouldn't come. Stony thanked the family for their cooperation and instructed them on how to write their witness statements. He then said the officers would assist them.

Lou had been silent throughout the ordeal. She looked content to stay where she was with her cameras capturing the aftermath. Fen caught her eye when he cleared his throat. "It's time for us to leave."

She responded by rolling her eyes. "Don't you know every story needs a strong ending? Readers will want to know what happens next."

Gil answered, "I do a fair amount of reading and know what you mean. There's something that's been a burr under my saddle for years. Prissy claims I got drunk in Las Vegas and married her. She even showed me what she claims is a marriage license. I believe it's a forgery. I need someone to go to Vegas with me who knows how to find things in a courthouse. What would you say to an all-expenses paid trip and a fat bonus for proving if I'm married to her or not?" He quickly added. "Separate rooms and no expectations of anything except going to a few shows and trying our luck at the tables. I like to be seen with a pretty woman on my arm. It brings me good luck."

Lou's eyes blinked like a bright light had caught her by surprise. She licked her lips and swallowed. "Will you answer any questions I might ask?"

"That sounds like a small price to pay to finally be free of that crazy woman." He grimaced. "Can you wait until these ribs heal to where I can get around without too much pain? After that, my life will be an open book."

"It's a deal," said Lou.

Fen thought everything was over, but Gil had something else to say. "As soon as everyone who isn't family clears out, I'd like my sons, June, and Ren to stay. It's time I started acting like a real father and mended some fences."

Ren moved to the center of the room, extended her arms, and spun in a circle.

Chapter Thirty-Four

The stacks of file folders on Chuck's desk hadn't diminished in the weeks since Fen returned from Georgetown. The attorney gave a quick glance at his wife, Candy, and opened a file. "Entertain the crime fighter while I read over this brief."

Candy blew out a huff of exasperation toward her husband and swiveled her head to Fen. "Excuse my husband's manners. He stayed up late watching basketball. You might notice that his voice is scratchy from hurling obscenities at the television."

Chuck shot a piercing gaze over the folder. "I'm not blaming the TV. It was the referees. I don't know how much someone paid them to rig the game, but..." His words slid into a puddle of mumbles. He then slammed the folder shut and threw it on top of a stack that was already leaning.

Candy shot to her feet in a valiant attempt to keep the stack upright. Too late. It slid into another stack. Like dominoes, the chain reaction continued. Chuck didn't help matters by jutting out both hands in an attempt to stop the avalanches. Piles squirted into one another and shot out all sides of the desktop.

This action left Candy and Chuck almost nose to nose, leaning over his massive desk. Fen couldn't get a good look at Candy, but the look on Chuck's face told him the attorney was no longer thinking about last night's basketball game.

Candy righted herself and placed her hands on her hips. "Leave it. We'll use the conference room for our meeting with Fen. After that, I'm filing all but five folders. Everything's being filed where they belong, and you won't say a word about it."

Chuck had no rebuttal. He grabbed his coffee cup and made for the door. Fen was only a step behind him. He'd never seen Candy in full meltdown mode and didn't want this to be the day.

Candy took her time, which gave Fen a few minutes to pour a warm-up in the small kitchen, make it to the conference room, and settle into a chair. He whispered to his attorney, "Will it be washing dishes for a week or sleeping on the couch?"

"The couch. Definitely the couch. Count the minutes before she joins us. It will be one night on the couch for each minute she keeps us waiting."

Fen grimaced. "Ouch. What's your record?"

"Thirty-two nights. It was for something much worse than knocking over files."

Candy entered the conference room six minutes later.

Chuck appeared content with his pending punishment and started the meeting as if nothing had happened. "How's Thelma these days?"

It amazed Fen how Chuck could free his mind from all troubles and focus on only one thing at a time.

"She's much better. The medicine for her hot flashes isn't miracle pills, but it's enough to where Bailey and I don't have to hide."

Chuck looked to be on the verge of a quip when Candy's

gaze plucked the words out of his mouth. He moved on. "And Bailey? Did helping you with the investigation satisfy her itch to become a P.I. for a while?"

"I'm not sure." That was a tough question for him to give a simple answer to. "I may be wrong, but Bailey's not been the same since we got back from Georgetown. She met a young deputy there. They went to a movie. Now they're talking and texting every day. It's not the first time a young man has turned her head, but this time seems different. I think she may go as far as enrolling in Southwestern University. They offer degrees in art and business."

"Do you think she'll finish a degree?" asked Candy.

Fen raised his shoulders and let them fall. "If you'd have asked me that a month ago, I'd have said no. Now, I'm not so sure. If this romance is a flash in the pan, then my answer will be a definite no." Fen interlaced his fingers and allowed his hands to rest on the table. "It's possible she'll get an apartment with her new friend, Ren Duvant. Bailey told Thelma that Ren wants to start classes in the fall. Her grandfather will foot the bill."

Chuck summarized. "A fellow female artist to live with, studying art and business, and a handsome young man to date sounds like enough to lure her away from Thelma's cooking."

"You might be right, but she runs hot and cold on making long-term commitments."

"It all depends on how you define long-term," said Candy. "For Bailey, one fall semester living with another girl would seem like a five-year commitment. That being said, I trust your instincts. It wouldn't surprise me if she tries another round of college, especially if there's a romance waiting for her."

Chuck placed his palms flat on the table. "Enough speculation. Have you heard from any of the Duvant family?"

"I'm staying in touch with the sheriff. He says Gil is loosening up the purse strings with Les and Robert. He's also given Chance permission to sell a five-hundred-acre tract of land and reinvest the proceeds in the ranch however he sees fit."

"What's Lou doing this week?" asked Chuck.

"She's in Vegas," said Fen. "She and Gil Duvant flew out three days ago. She's been searching their courthouse records by day and going to shows at night. There's no official proof Gil and Prissy were ever married."

Candy cleared her throat. "I can update that report. The police searched Prissy's home when animal control came to get the dogs. There's a marriage license, but Sheriff Stony says it's a forgery. He's working on Prissy to admit it."

"What else did the sheriff tell you that he didn't tell me?" asked Fen.

Chuck cut in. "That's about it. Stony is happy as a cat with a bowl of cream."

Fen huffed through his nose. "Even though I didn't complete the job?"

Confusion swept across Chuck's face. "What are you talking about? You did what we asked you to do, and more. We sent you to Williamson County to see if Gilbert Duvant died in an accidental house fire, or if someone killed him. You did that then discovered the two women who killed him and tried to kill Gil."

Chuck took a breath. "When did you know it was a homicide?"

"I had a hunch all along, but it was when the guys in white coats didn't find the remains of a dog that light bulbs went off in my brain. Billy wouldn't have left Gilbert and would have done all he could to protect him. It also made me look hard at Prissy. She knew Billy well enough for him to trust her. Eventually, I realized both Prissy and Sunny were after land. Prissy was obsessed with building and operating a pet cemetery. Sunny wanted land to develop."

Fen dipped his head in shame. "That's where I didn't finish what I should have." He raised his head and looked at Candy then Chuck. "I caught the two who killed Gilbert Duvant, which is the good news. The bad news is I didn't catch the one who planned everything. He's still running free."

Both Chuck and Candy sat still. Candy was the first to speak. "We weren't for sure about that. How did you realize someone else was behind the curtain pulling the levers?"

"It happened when I finally hit flow state while painting. Prissy admitted to me she thinks and reacts more like an animal than a human, but I didn't fully believe her. No matter how much she wanted a pet cemetery, she couldn't kill Gilbert or Gil, but she could help someone else do it."

"What about Sunny?" asked Chuck.

"Bart Hill had her eating out of his hand. I don't believe there's anything she wouldn't have done for him."

"Wait," said Chuck. "Are you saying Bart Hill planned the killing and the attempted murder?"

Fen nodded. "I don't know if Sunny would have come up with it by herself, but with Bart whispering in her ear his big plans for the two of them, I think it wasn't too hard to convince her. And Prissy was the perfect partner in crime. Sunny couldn't lure Gilbert out of his house, but Prissy could. Prissy couldn't kill Gilbert or rig the home for a gas explosion and fire, but Sunny could. Prissy couldn't take the shot at Gil, but Sunny could. I really believe Prissy never knew Bart was pulling the strings. Only Sunny knew, who was over the moon in love with him."

Chuck then asked, "Does Stony know about Bart Hill?"

Candy spoke up. "Of course he does. So do the Texas Rangers, the FBI, and the IRS."

The lawyer's eyebrows shot up. "How do you know?"

"Because I'm smart enough not to stack files on my desk until they fall over, and I know how Fen thinks and acts. He's already hatched a plan to have others finish the job for him. They may not get Mr. Hill for murder or attempted murder, but they'll make his life so miserable he'll look forward to going to jail."

Fen stood. "Thanks for the coffee and the visit. Come out to see me. Thelma's developed a new recipe for cookies."

Named the Red Poppy Capital of Texas, Georgetown has come a long way from the days when cattle were driven along the Chisholm Trail through the middle of downtown. It is now a prime Texas getaway location.

One of the many wonderful advantages we enjoy today are the coffee shops which have sprung up. JUST LOVE COFFEE CAFE, where Fen and Les met for breakfast, is a real coffee shop where I spent many an hour writing this book. The owner kindly gave me permission to use the cafe's name. I hope you'll stop in sometime for a cup of coffee and a Flying Pig.

If you enjoyed this book, please consider leaving a review at your favorite retailer, Bookbub or Goodreads.

To get in on the fun in my reader community, scan below or go to brucehammack.com/the-fen-maguire-mysteries-prequel/ to join my mailing list and receive a free copy of the series prequel, *Murder On Shinbone Creek*.

Happy Reading!
Bruce

Drawing from his extensive background in criminal justice, Bruce Hammack writes contemporary, clean read detective and crime mysteries. A huge fan of Hercule Poirot and Sherlock Holmes, he believes the world can never have enough whodunits!

He is the author of the Smiley and McBlythe Mysteries, the Fen Maguire Mysteries and the Star of Justice series. Having lived in eighteen cities around the world, he now shares his home in the Texas hill country with his wife of thirty-plus years.

Follow Bruce on Amazon, Bookbub and Goodreads for the latest new release info and recommendations. Learn more at brucehammack.com.